Eli Thayer

Six Speeches

With a sketch of the life of Hon. Eli Thayer

Eli Thayer

Six Speeches
With a sketch of the life of Hon. Eli Thayer

ISBN/EAN: 9783337011758

Printed in Europe, USA, Canada, Australia, Japan

Cover: Foto ©Raphael Reischuk / pixelio.de

More available books at **www.hansebooks.com**

SIX SPEECHES

WITH A

SKETCH OF THE LIFE

OF

HON. ELI THAYER.

———

BOSTON:
BROWN AND TAGGARD.
1860.

SIX SPEECHES

OF

HON. ELI THAYER.

["Welcome evermore to gods and men," says Emerson, "is the *self-helping* man. For him all doors are flung wide; him all tongues greet, all honors crown, all eyes follow with desire."

He who shows that he can do without our help, is exactly the man whose help we cannot do without. The self-helper helps all the rest, because he shows them of what they are capable. When the virgin soil of Kansas was given over to the foul embrace of slavery, and they who might have saved it desponded when they should have done nothing but labor, one man, with no public record hitherto, applied his quick brain to the problem, and his stout heart to the work,—and straightway the thing despaired of was done! That man was ELI THAYER, of Massachusetts. The struggle between free and slave labor was protracted far beyond the necessary limit, and was likely, at last, to be decided in favor of slavery. Not that the latter really possessed larger power, but it happened that it was already on the ground, was familiar with the field, could cope successfully with frontier obstacles, and enjoyed the strong prestige of never yet having been beaten in such an encounter. It bade fair, at that time, to worry Freedom out, and the field had already been virtually abandoned by the friends of the latter, who were retiring in a sullen and angry mood from the conflict. All that was needed, at that particular crisis, was organization. The Free-State men were secretly conscious of their superior strength, yet knew not how to wield it. The right elements were to be had, but the master spirit was wanting, who should skilfully combine them. And, just at the right moment, that spirit stepped forth,

—a new man to the masses, but himself thoroughly conscious of the power he held in his hand.

That man was ELI THAYER, of Massachusetts, and his secret was ORGANIZED EMIGRATION. Nobody, apparently, had thought of it,—the simplest thing in the world. And yet it was like a new discovery in the social development of the century, whose influence is to work until the whole earth is colonized, and the dreams of universal brotherhood are finally made real. For by this single agency all uninhabited quarters of the globe are capable of smiling with the presence of a dense population. The work of the lonely pioneer has come to an end. We shall call on no more solitary hunters, like Daniel Boone, to wander forth from the extreme verge of civilized life and lose himself in the yellow sunset, for a whole town, county, and State may be transported as by magic; the surplus of a dense population, by this simple machinery, being planted in the heart of wildernesses almost by the sheer force and play of the single will that sets the machinery in operation.

It is conceded that Eli Thayer, whatever else he may receive credit for, has earned the name of the originator of Organized Emigration: a system whose wonderful effects will be felt years after he is dead, and for which future generations will bless his name. It was Eli Whitney, another New England man, whose fertile brain invented the wonder called the Cotton Gin; but, for ourselves, great as cotton is, and is yet to be, we would far rather enjoy the honor of having invented the machine by which free labor may go and colonize wherever it will, with the assurance

of its enjoying its honest reward. The benefits of association, in one form and another,
had already been advertised to the world, as
in the case of banking, building, and insuring,
but we had yet to see the same principle applied to colonization, and work out its magic
results with such marvellous certainty and
rapidity. Now, we may remove from the
Atlantic to the Pacific coast an entire town
at a time, carrying out with us our favorite
schools, churches, trades, and callings, none
of which need part with their precious asso-
ciations by the removal. This makes the no-
madic a civilized life, tents being exchanged
for houses. And nothing is more certain,
than that where a people feels such rapid
transmigration possible, all hopes of subduing
their spirit or alienating their love for freedom
are vain indeed.

As a fit introduction to the public speeches
in Congress of the man who first taught us
how to apply the system of Emigration to the
spread of free labor over the continent, a
brief sketch of his personal career may not
be without interest to readers everywhere.
The public would know all they can about a
man of mark, nor ought he to expect to con-
ceal himself. Fortunately, however, no one
can impute to Eli Thayer a necessity for being at all fastidious about the most public
showing of his entire career. It is of charac-
teristic interest enough to be sought out for
publication in an European journal like the
London Times, which thus helps to send his
name, with a clear and true ring, quite around
the world. That powerful journal, no doubt,
regards him, to borrow the expression of one
of our own leading presses, "as the chief in-
terpreter of the great agencies which science
and invention have placed within the grasp
of man, and with which not only is the physical world to be subdued to its uses, but false
systems and oppressive institutions, founded
in fraud, are to be crushed out of existence."

Mr. Thayer is a native of Mendon, Mass.,
where he was born in the year 1819. His
father was a laborious farmer, and subse-
quently kept a country store in that part of
the town now known as Blackstone. He was
unable to do any thing for his son Eli, more
than other men in similarly cramped situa-
tions, and the lad was therefore kept at work
on the farm till he was well grown, obtaining
such meagre instruction as the district school
of that day afforded him. But he was of an
active turn of mind, and had learned enough
to become eager to know more. About the
time he had exhausted the rudiments in the
district school, his father failed in business;
but that hindered the lad none in his plans.
He resolved to acquire a liberal education,
and one day informed his father of his determination. How he was going to accomplish
his end was not much more clear to the mind
of the one than the other. It was in the
year 1835 when he packed his few clothes
and placed his trunk on board a boat on the
Blackstone Canal, bound for Worcester, and
himself walked the entire distance. Such
was his first entry into the city whose best
interests he was so soon afterwards to subserve.

In Worcester, he entered the "Manual
Labor School," an institution that furnished
indigent young men, who might be so inclined,
with a chance to pay for their schooling in
work, as they went along. In this school
young Thayer fitted himself for College,
never having known a syllable either of
Latin or Greek previous to coming here.
After a year's hard labor and study, pursued
night and day with restless energy, he presented himself for admission into Brown University, at Providence. In mathematical at-
tainments he was found deficient, not coming
up to the standard; but on his solemn promise, that, by persevering labor, he would
"catch up" and hold his place, under the
circumstances of the case, he was admitted;
and the promise was remembered with pride
by his instructor when he came to leave the
walls of his honored alma mater, for Thayer
was the best in mathematics of his class.

Eli Thayer entered college with nothing,
and graduated with distinguished honors, and
a few hundred dollars in his pocket. That
is more than many of our college graduates
can say. While in the University, he de-
frayed his expenses by teaching district
schools during the intervals of vacations, and
by similar labors, from time to time, to those
which sustained him at the school in Worcester. He played the carpenter, the wood-
sawyer, and the landscape gardener; and
there is a piece of embankment before one of
the Professors' residences to-day, the green
sods of which he placed with his own hands;
and they were well placed, too. Such a
young man cannot fail to make his mark in
the world of men in time, the supply being

yet too scanty not to quicken the demand, when they do appear.

On leaving college, he returned to Worcester, and was made Principal of the very school in which he had been qualified for the University, the same being now known as the "Worcester Academy." Here he worked on as few men do work, even in the high vocation of teacher; and in the year 1851, he opened a school for girls on what was known as Goat's Hill, in a noble and appropriate structure which his own enterprise had erected. Several acres are connected with the building, and the spot was named Mount Oread. The "Oread Institute," with its numerous pupils and its corps of skilful and accomplished teachers, enjoys a fame, as wide as Worcester herself, throughout the country. Mr. Thayer actively superintended the entire education of his pupils; and, even now, finds time enough to carry on his original design with all the industry and vigor which he first brought to its development.

Previous to entering on this undertaking, however, Mr. Thayer interested himself largely in real estate enterprises; and it is notorious that the city of Worcester is, to-day, indebted as much to him as to any other man for opening up certain leading improvements, such as locating shops and factories and mills, that have given an abiding impulse to its growth and material prosperity. It is not necessary to describe the Oread Institute; every stranger who passes through Worcester, in the cars, at once espies it and makes particular inquiry about it. Its towers, its long line of masonry, forming a sort of apronwork from end to end, its battlements and its imposing position, attract immediate attention, and are worthy to crown a spot that of itself forms one of the boldest features of the town. It is proper to add that this seminary is well sustained by the public far and near, furnishing its projector with a liberal and certain income, as his enterprise well deserves.

While still engaged in the business of instruction, he has found time to indulge his tastes, to a greater or less degree, for politics. He always took a profound interest in public questions, and was ready with his opinions — intelligent, well-considered and independent, — when called upon for their expression. In this regard, he furnishes a fine example of what really belongs to every good citizen, not to be so indifferent to all other pursuits than his own, as to lead a life of selfishness and seclusion, but to hold himself ready to give his fellow-citizens the benefit of his aid and counsel in any emergency. Thus he has been an Alderman in his adopted city. During the winter of 1853-4, he served as a member of the Massachusetts Legislature, from Worcester, and again in the following winter. In this capacity he gave his political friends and supporters abundant satisfaction by his services.

It was during his last term as a legislator that those events were born in our national history, which require just such a man to unravel and master them. The famous Kansas-Nebraska Bill having passed Congress, by the consequent repeal of the long-standing Missouri Compromise the young territories were forthwith thrown open for a hand-to-hand struggle between the forces of Free and Slave Labor. Whichever should win in that fight, was to possess those lands for all time. The Free State men were at a distance; their opponents were already, as it were, on the ground. The former were placed at a still greater disadvantage, that they either had to pass directly through a slave State to reach Kansas, or to make a circuitous and wearisome journey further to the north, through a free State. It was expensive to remove all the way to Kansas; little was known of the country at the East; men were extremely loth to take their families, one by one, so far beyond the frontier; and, with such a variety and force of opposition, the spirit of the friends of Free Labor began sensibly to flag, even while they saw and lamented that the prize might, with proper effort, be won. How to make that effort most effective was the problem.

Eli Thayer sat in the State Capitol and thought the whole thing out. He caught the spirit of the hour, and conceived the magic plan that was to bring order out of chaos, dissipate the fears of the lovers of freedom, and rescue a young State from the curse, whose dark shadow was then passing over its plains. On the instant, he made known his plan. By many it was lightly thought of, because it was so simple. Others would rather wait to see how it was likely to work. The doubters were as plenty as they always are at such times. But Mr. Thayer possessed a wonderful power of *work*; and, as an Englishman would say, work generally accomplishes the end sought for.

The first step he took was to procure the charter of an "Emigrant Aid Society" from the Legislature, having already enlisted the sympathy and co-operation of many of the leading men of the State. To show that this movement was, in no sense, a political, but rather a social and economic one, from the start, it is sufficient to state, that among the original corporators to whom this grant was made by the Legislature, appear the names of Col. Isaac Davis, of Worcester; and Gen. J. S. Whitney, of Springfield. Hon. A. A. Lawrence, of Boston, likewise lent it his aid in a large and effective amount of ready money, as is well remembered by all.

Having obtained his charter, the next step to be pursued by Mr. Thayer was to excite and direct public sentiment in favor of his plan. The people wanted nothing so much as to make Kansas a free State, but they were in the dark about the *modus operandi*. If they could be convinced that there was a way by which they could compass their ardent desire, they would seize hold of it without any hesitation. To enlist the confidence of men everywhere in his project, — the grand project of Organized Emigration, — Mr. Thayer left home and business, and perseveringly gave himself to the work of elucidating his scheme before the people and pressing it home to their convictions. While engaged in this labor, —for it was indeed labor, — he travelled thousands of miles and addressed hundreds of meetings, holding conferences with inquiring men at all places and points within his reach, and preaching, without intermission, his theory that organized free labor could easily overthrow organized slave labor, if the experiment was once but fairly tried. In good time, he beheld his work prosper. Emigrants began to flock around the standard he had so boldly erected in large numbers. They rallied, not as a mob, but in disciplined ranks and masses. From the offices of emigration, which were established at different points, parties were forwarded straight to the ground in dispute, one following close at the heels of another, all of them orderly and resolute, all bent on fulfilling the destiny of actual settlers; and, taken as a whole, the finest specimen of emigrating valor and virtue ever seen in history. It was indeed, to look back upon it now, a wonderful feat for the brain of a single man to accomplish.

The various parties of Free-State settlers began now to pour into Kansas without interruption. In a very brief period of time, many thousands of persons—the flower of our States—were securely established on the soil, having staked out their claims and become real residents and owners. Had this work been deferred until the next spring only, Kansas would have been lost, by universal admission; for the Missouri lodges were organizing as rapidly as possible, and it was the design of the prime movers in the plan to throw them across the line into the Territory in dispute, just as soon as the next season opened. In that case, it would have been idle for the men of the north and the east to start at all; their labor would have come to nought even before it was begun. The secret of the free-labor success was, that by the rapidity and compactness of its emigration, under the scheme of Eli Thayer, the work was done before the other side had time to think of it. They invited a free contest, and they were beaten. The intended crossing over the line, on the following spring, was not undertaken. The battle had clearly gone against them. This they confessed by their acts of retaliatory violence and their loud expressions of indignation. So incensed were they, even before the deed was known to be done, they offered a reward for the head of Eli Thayer, the author and inventor of the scheme by which their game was thus blocked, and kept the reward standing for some time at the head of their newspapers! Had they secured his caput, they would have been likely to obtain a good deal more than they bargained for. He would have taught them a practical point in the art of emigration, far beyond any they yet knew. *Their* plan was based on force, absolute and brutal; Thayer sent forward the saw-mill and grist-mill as *his* pioneer, and men followed close after steam. Davy Atchison, seeing one of these steam mills passing on one day, remarked, with an oath, to a friend standing by, "There goes another Yankee city!" And he was right. The steam mill drew a whole township close behind it, including a school, a church, and a newspaper; and this was Eli Thayer's fortunate and timely discovery.

The result in Kansas having proved so auspicious to Free Labor, the attention of

Mr. Thayer's fellow citizens was afterwards drawn to him as a peculiarly fit man to represent them in Congress. Judge Chapin happened to be the nominee of the party, and had accepted the nomination; only eight days before the election, however, he felt compelled, for good reasons, to decline the position. This left the Republicans of the Worcester district in a bad plight; and, for the moment, it seemed as if there was no chance of defeating Col. DeWitt, the deservedly popular candidate of the Americans. Many despaired and would give up the battle; but a few determined to go on and make another nomination. Mr. Eli Thayer was at once waited on by the Committee to whom Mr. Chapin's resignation had been sent, and asked if he would consent to run in his place. "Yes," was the ready and decisive answer. They reminded him how short the time was to election day, and told him what kind of work, and how much of it, he would be expected to perform, in order to secure success. This only excited his courage the more. "Furnish me with facilities for travelling through the district," said Mr. Thayer, "and I will be ready to speak four times in every twenty-four hours!" The Committee were surprised. They promised, however, to do their part. It is a matter of political history that Eli Thayer did his; and he made nothing of putting twenty miles between his afternoon and first evening addresses. He was all game, and all endurance. It was simply impossible to defeat such a man, for no other could hold out against him.

He was triumphantly elected to Congress by the people of his district, and entered upon his duties as a national legislator, in December of the year 1857. His entrance upon the floor of the House attracted much attention, for all were eager to see the man whose single idea had been the instrument of redeeming Kansas from the hands of her enemies. Probably many men then thought that the price set on his head was altogether *too low*.

His first speech in Congress was delivered on the 7th of January, 1858, on the Central American Question. All sides agreed that it produced a decided sensation. It was off the beaten track of Congressional discussion and disclosed a vein of freshness, originality, and humor that was not looked for. The New York *Tribune* said of it, that "by com-mon consent, it established Mr. Thayer's fame." His object, in the speech, was to hint a plan for organized emigration from the North to Nicaragua,— in other words, for "Americanizing Central America." It produced such a surprise among those men from the Gulf States who think that Central America belongs exclusively to their own bailiwick, that they were puzzled, for a time, whether to laugh or swear. It was said that so rich a scene is rarely witnessed in Congress as presented itself during the delivery of that speech. Without remarking any further upon it, it is given herewith exactly as it was reported].

Mr. Thayer said:—

MR. CHAIRMAN,— It is my purpose to offer an amendment to the resolution which is now before the Committee, for the purpose of widening the proposed investigation. I do not intend to discuss at all the topics which the Committee has been considering during the past three days. I am not here to consider whether Mr. Walker was legally or illegally arrested, or whether Commodore Paulding is to be censured or applauded for his action. I shall express no sympathy with the course pursued by the President. I have no intention to discuss his position in relation to this matter, neither is it my purpose to enter the lists with the gentleman from Tennessee [Mr. Maynard], who eulogized the heroism of Mr. Walker — a man, who, claiming to be the President of Nicaragua, and to represent in his own person the sovereignty of that State, surrendered without a protest, and without a blow, to a power upon his own soil, which he claimed to be an invading force. Whether this be heroism, I shall not now inquire.

I thrust aside, for the present, all questions of legal technicality in this matter; all the mysteries of the construction of the neutrality laws; all these questions which have engrossed the attention of the House during the last three days, and concerning which everybody has been speaking, and nobody caring; and I. come to that great, paramount, transcendent question, about which everybody is caring and nobody is speaking: "How shall we Americanize Central America?"

It may be a matter of surprise that I pass

over two or three questions which, in their natural order, seem to be antecedent to this one. And these questions are: First, Do we *wish* to Americanize Central America? Secondly, *Can* we Americanize Central America? Thirdly, *Shall* we Americanize Central America?

Now, Mr. Chairman, I say that whoever has studied the history of this country, and whoever knows the character of this people, and whoever can infer their destiny from their character and their history, knows that these three preliminary questions are already answered by the American people — that we *do wish* to Americanize Central America; that we *can* Americanize Central America; and that we *shall* Americanize Central America.

And now, Mr. Chairman, in relation to the manner and agency. *How* can we Americanize Central America? Shall we do it legally and fairly, or illegally and unfairly? Shall we do it by conferring a benefit on the people of Central America, or shall we do it by conquest, by robbery, and violence? Shall we do it without abandoning national laws, and without violating our treaty stipulations? Shall we do it in accordance with the law of nations and the laws of the United States, or shall we do it by force, blood, and fire?

Now, Mr. Chairman, my position is this: that we will do it legally; that we will do it in accordance with the highest laws, human and divine.

By the way, sir, I did agree with the gentleman from New York [Mr. Haskin], when he told us yesterday that he was not in favor of petit larceny; but I did not agree with him when he said he was in favor of grand larceny. I regret that a Representative of the people of the United States, in the Council Hall of the nation, should say to his constituents, to the nation, and to the world, that he and the Democratic party were "rather in favor of grand larceny." Larceny is *larceny;* and you cannot say a meaner thing about it than to call it by its own name. I am pained that this report has gone forth, that any party, or that any individual in this House, or connected with this Government, is in favor of grand larceny or petit larceny. Larceny, grand or petit, is not only disgraceful, but is absolutely and utterly contemptible. We do not go for the acquisition or Americanization of territory by larceny of any kind whatever, but fairly, openly, and honorably.

Then, sir, by what agency may we thus Americanize Central America? I reply to the question, by the power of organized emigration. That is abundantly able to give us Central America as soon as we want it. We could have Americanized Central America half a dozen times by this power within the last three years, if there had been no danger or apprehension of meddlesome or vexatious Executive interference. But if we are to use this mighty power of organized emigration, we want a different kind of neutrality laws from those which we now have; and, therefore, I am desirous that this Committee shall recommend something which shall not subject us to the misconstruction of the President of the United States, or to his construction at all. I want these neutrality laws so plain that every man may know whether he is in the right or in the wrong, whether he is violating those laws or is not violating them. For, Mr. Chairman, with our new-fashioned kind of emigration, with our organized emigration, which goes in colonies, and therefore must, of necessity, to some extent, resemble a military organization, there is great danger that a President with a dim intellect may make a mistake, and subject to harassing and vexatious delays, and sometimes to loss and injury, a peaceful, quiet colony, going out to settle in a neighboring State.

Mr. Chairman, I can illustrate this position. You, sir, remember that in the year 1856, when it was *bad travelling* across the State of Missouri, on the way to Kansas, our colonies went through the State of Iowa, and through the Territory of Nebraska. These were peaceful, quiet colonies, going to settle in the Territory of Kansas, by that long and wearisome journey, because it was *bad travelling* through the State of Missouri. You remember that one of these colonies of organized emigrants, which went from Maine and Massachusetts, and from various other Northern States, was arrested just as it was passing over the southern boundary of the Territory of Nebraska, on its way to its future home in Kansas. It was a peaceful, quiet colony, going out with its emigrant wagons, "all in a row," and, therefore, looking something like a military organization; going out with their women and their children, with sub-soil plows with coulters a yard long [laughter], with pick-axes, with crowbars, with shovels, and with garden seeds. This beautiful colony was arrested by the officials of the present Executive's predecessor. It was by some mistake, no doubt. Perhaps he took the turnip-seed for powder; and I doubt whether the case would have been better if the President had been there himself. This colony was arrested within our own dominion. It was not an emigration to a foreign country, and there was no danger of interference with the neutrality laws. These quiet, peaceful colonists, because their wagons went in a row for mutual defence, through the wild, uncultivated Territory of Nebraska, where there were Indians, they were arrested as a military organization. We do not want, hereafter, either within the limits of the United States or without them, any such meddlesome and vexatious interference by the executive power of this Government. Therefore, I say, let us have some neutrality laws that can be understood. If there had been no apprehensions in the North about the neutrality laws, if we had not expected that whatever emigration we might have fitted out for Central America would have been arrested within the marine league of the harbor of Boston, why, we would have colonized Central America years ago, and had it ready for admission into the Union before this time. We want a modification or an elucidation of the neutrality laws, and I trust that it will be the duty of the committee so to report.

Before I proceed to consider the power and benefits of this system of organized emigration, and the reason why it ought not to be rejected by this House, I will proceed, as briefly as I can, to show the interests which the Northern portion of this country has in Americanizing Central America, as contrasted with the interests which the Southern portion has in doing the same thing. I come, then, to speak of the immense interests which the Northern States have in this proposed enterprise. I am astonished, that so far in this debate the advocates for Americanizing Central America seem to be mostly from those States which border on the Gulf of Mexico. As yet, I have heard no man from the Northern States advocating the same thing. Let us look at the interests of the Northern States in this question, and then at those of the Southern States.

These Northern States are, as the States of Northern Europe were designated by Tacitus. *officina gentium.* "the manufactory of nations." We can make one state a year. In the last three years we have colonized almost wholly the Territory of Kansas. We have furnished settlers to Minnesota and Nebraska, and the Lord knows where, but we have not exhausted one-half of our natural increase. We have received accessions to our numbers in that time, from foreign countries, of more than one million of souls, and now we have no relief; we are worse off to-day than we were when we began to colonize Kansas. We must have an outlet somewhere for our surplus population. [Laughter.]

Sir, I have a resolution in my pocket, which I have been carrying about for days, waiting patiently for an opportunity to present it in this House, instructing the Committee on Territories to report a bill organizing and opening for settlement the Indian Territory. Mr. Chairman, I came to this conclusion with reluctance, that we must have the Indian Territory. But necessity knows no law. We must go somewhere. Something must be opened to the descendants of the Pilgrims. [Laughter.] Why, sir, just look at it. We are crammed in between the Atlantic and Pacific Oceans. The bounding billows of our emigration are dashing fiercely against both sides of the Rocky Mountains. Obstructed now by these barriers, this westward moving tide begins to set back. Will it flow towards Canada? Not at all. It has already begun to flow over the "Old Dominion" [laughter], and into other States. Missouri is almost inundated with it. We cannot check this tide of flowing emigration. You might as well try to shut out from this continent, by curtains, the light of the aurora borealis. No such thing can be accomplished. This progress must be onward, and we *must* have territory. We must have territory; and I think it most opportune that the proposition seems to be before the country to Americanize Central America. A better time could not be; for, in addition to the population which we now have, which is immense in the Northern States, as I shall show you in proceeding, this financial pressure in the East, and in the different nations of Europe, will send to our shores in the year 1858 not less than half a million of men. In addition to that we have two hundred and fifty thousand of our own population, who will change localities in that time. Then, sir, there are seven hundred and fifty thousand men to be prepared for, somewhere, in the year 1858—men enough, sir, to make eight States, if we only had Territories in which to put them, and if we only use them economically [laughter], as we are sure to do by this system of organized emigration.

Now, could any thing be more opportune, at this time, than to have this project submitted to us, of opening Central America to settlement? I assure you, if the Committee will report any bill which will enable the people of the North, without larceny of any kind, without tyranny of any kind, to settle that country, I will postpone my resolution for the opening of the Indian Territory, at least until the next session of Congress.

But it is not only for the purpose of furnishing an outlet for our immense population in the North that I now advocate the Americanizing of Central America. The interests of commerce, as well as this great argument of necessity, are on our side. Who has the trade beyond Central America? We have whale fisheries in the Northern Ocean, which build up great cities upon the eastern shore of Massachusetts. We have trade with Oregon and California, with the Sandwich Islands, and the western coast of South America. We are opening a trade, destined to be an immense trade, with the Empires of China and Japan, and we must of necessity have in Central America certain factors and certain commercial agencies, who, in a very few years, with their families and relatives and dependants, will make a dense population in Central America. I say, then, that for the interests of commerce we want Central America Americanized. This commercial interest is, unfortunately, a sectional interest in these States. It is, emphatically, a Northern interest; and therefore, as a Northern man, I advocate especially that Central America should be Americanized.

Now, sir, I said I was astonished that gentlemen who come from States bordering upon the Gulf, had advocated this project, and not the Representatives who come from Northern States. Let us see the reason why the North should be more zealous than the South in this movement. In the State of Massachusetts we have one hundred and twenty-seven people to a square mile, by the census of 1850. In the State of Rhode Island we have one hundred and twelve to the square mile, by

the same census. In the State of Connecticut we have seventy-nine. In the State of New York we have sixty-five. So, you see, it was not fiction, it was not poetry, not a stretch of the imagination, when I told you that the descendants of the Pilgrims were in a tight place. [Laughter.]

But how is it with the States which border upon the Gulf? Look at it and see. They have, some of them, eighty-nine hundredths of a man to the square mile. [Laughter.] In another one we have one and the forty-eight hundredth part of a man to the square mile; and, taking them altogether, we have just about three men to the square mile in all those States which border upon the Gulf of Mexico.

Now, sir, it would be folly for me to argue, and there is no kind of reason for supposing, that these States expect to do any thing about colonizing Central America. They cannot afford to lose a man. They had better give away two thousand dollars than to lose a single honest, industrious citizen. They cannot afford it. I have left out of this calculation, to be sure, the enumeration of the slaves in those States, for the gentleman from Tennessee [Mr. Maynard] informed us that the question of Slavery did not come into this argument properly, and I agree with him there. I think he may agree with me, that by no possibility can slavery ever be established in Central America. That is my belief. Just fix your neutrality laws, and we will fill up Central America before 1860 sufficiently to be comfortable.

Mr. MAYNARD. With the permission of the gentleman, I desire to ask him whether he will pledge himself for his constituents, and for all those he represents, that when they get down there they will not make slaves of the people they find there?

Mr. THAYER. Certainly I will do it; and I will say more on that subject hereafter. I will say to the gentlemen upon the other side who have advocated this right of emigration, and have no personal interest in this matter, that they can have no pecuniary interest in it, for they have no men to spare for this enterprise. And especially do I honor the gentleman from Mississippi [Mr. Quitman], who professed to be moved by arguments of philanthropy in relation to this question, and who maintained that the people of Central America were oppressed, that they needed our assistance, and that it was conferring a benefit upon them to send out colonies among them to aid them to get rid of their oppressors. This is more than patriotism. It approaches universal brotherhood. I am glad that that gentleman is defending the rights of emigration. No man prizes those rights more highly than I do. I think that I understand their power and their value, and I am glad to welcome among the list of political regenerators, the gentleman from Mississippi with such large, wide, and noble views upon this question. I do not here endorse his whole speech. I did not hear the whole of it. I do not know what he said about Mr. Walker, whether he defends him, or whether he does not. For myself, I do not say that I defend him, or that I do not, at this time. I wait for the report of our committee, to know what are the facts in this case, and whether he is fit to be defended or not.

Now, sir, I am rejoiced that I have found aid and comfort in a great political missionary movement from a quarter where I least expected it. This argument of philanthropy is sufficiently potent with the South; while I will not deny that it is always more or less potent with the North, perhaps not so potent with the North as with the South — very likely we are more material and less spiritual — but still, I say, it has some power at the North. We do not live so near the sun as do those gentlemen who border on the Gulf; but we live near enough to the sun to have some warmth in our hearts, and the appeals of philanthropy to us are not made in vain.

But, in addition to that, just look at it, sir! In addition to that great argument of philanthropy, we have not only the argument of necessity, but the argument of making money; and when you take those three arguments, and combine them, you make a great motive power, which is sufficient, in ordinary cases, to move Northern men, though they are not very mobile nor very fickle.

So much, Mr. Chairman, for the comparison of interests between the Northern and Southern people of these United States in relation to the Americanizing of Central America.

I come now to discuss, briefly, the power and benefits of this new mode of emigration. And, sir, what is its power? I tell you its power is greater than that which is wielded by any potentate or emperor upon the face

of God's footstool. If we can form a company, or a number of companies, which can control the emigration of this country, — the foreign emigration and native emigration, — I tell you, sir, that that company, or those companies, will have more power than any potentate or emperor upon the face of the earth; and that company, or those companies, may laugh at politicians; they may laugh, sir, at the President and his Cabinet; at the Supreme Court, and at Congress; for all these powers of the Government, great and mighty as they are, can do nothing, in accordance with the Constitution of this land, which can in any way interfere with our progress, or prevent our making cities, and states, and nations, wherever and whenever we please. Then, sir, there can be no doubt about the power of this agency, which, I tell you, is the right one for us to make use of in getting Central America if we want it, or in Americanizing Central America, as we are sure to do.

Now, Mr. Chairman, I have said nothing about annexing Central America to the United States. For myself, I care nothing about it, and I do not know whether the people of this country are ready for that proposition yet. I think, however, they would rather annex a thousand square leagues of territory than to lose a single square foot. To be sure, sir, we have a few men in the North who honestly hate this Union. I will not criticise their views. I will not condemn them for their views. They have a right to cherish just what views they please in relation to this question. Sir, there are still a larger number of sour and disappointed politicians, who, though they do not profess hatred to this Union, do, to a certain extent, profess indifference as to its continuance. But the great and overwhelming majority of the people of the North, sir, as a unit, are determined that *no force*, internal or external, shall ever wrest from the jurisdiction of the United States a single square foot of our territory, unless it first be baptized in blood and fire. That is the sentiment of the great majority of the people of the North, — that no portion of the territory of this Government shall ever be released from our possession. We understand that this Union is a partnership for life, and that the bonds that hold us together cannot by any fatuity be sundered until this great Government is first extinguished and its power annihilated. That, sir, is our sentiment about the Union, and such may be the present sentiment about annexation. But I have no doubt what the future sentiment of the country will be about annexation. I have no doubt we will have Central America in this Government, and all between this and Central America also.

Well, sir, we have now come to the grand missionary age of the world, in which we do not send our preachers alone, perplexing people who are in ignorance and barbarism with abstract theological dogmas; but with the preachers we send the church, we send the school, we send the mechanic and the farmer; we send all that makes up great and flourishing communities; we send the powers that build cities; we send steam-engines, sir, which are the greatest apostles of liberty that this country has ever seen. That is the modern kind of missionary emigration, and it has wonderful power on this continent, and is destined to have on the world, too, for it is just as good against one kind of evil as another; and it can just as well be exerted against idol worship in Hindostan and China, as against oppression and despotism in Central America.

But we take the countries that are nearest first; and now we propose to use this mighty power in originating a nation in quick time for Central America. We read of a time when "a nation shall be born in a day." I think it may be done in some such way as this. By this method of emigration the pioneer does not go into the wilderness

"*Alone*, unfriended, melancholy, slow,
Dragging at each remove a length'ning chain,"

stealing away from the institutions of religion and education, himself and family; but Christianity herself goes hand in hand with the pioneer; and not Christianity alone, but the offspring of Christianity, an awakened intelligence, and all the inventions of which she is the mother; creating all the differences between an advanced and enlightened community and one in degradation and ignorance. Sir, in years gone by, our emigration has ever tended toward barbarism; but now, by this method, it is tending to a higher civilization than we have ever witnessed. Why, sir, by this plan, a new community starts on as high a plane as the old one had ever arrived at; and leaving behind the dead and decayed branches which encumbered the old, with the vigorous energies of youth it presses on and ascends. Sir, such a State will be the State of Kansas, eclipsing in its progress all the other States of this nation, because it was colonized in this way. The people, in this way, have not to serve half a century of probation in semi-barbarism. They begin with schools and churches, and you will see what the effect is upon communities that are so established.

But I will speak now of that which constitutes the peculiar strength of emigration of this kind; and that is *the profit of the thing*. I have shown you how efficient it is, and I will now show you how the method works, to some extent. It is profitable for every one connected with it; it is profitable to the people where the colonies go; it is profitable to the people of the colonies; and it is profitable to the company, which is the guiding star and the protecting power of the colonies. It does good everywhere. It does evil nowhere.

Sir, you cannot resist a power like this. A good man often feels regret when he knows that by promoting a good cause he is at the same time sacrificing his own means of doing good, and is becoming weaker and weaker every day. It is a great drawback upon beneficent enterprises, even upon philanthropic and Christian enterprises, that the men who sustain them are lessening their own means of doing good by it. Sir, it is a great mistake to suppose that a good cause can only be sustained by the life-blood of its friends. But when a man can do a magnanimous act, when he can do a decidedly good thing, and at the same time make money by it, all his faculties are in harmony. [Laughter.] You do not need any great argument to induce men to take such a position, if you can only induce them to believe that such is the effect. Well, sir, such is the effect; and now let us apply it to the people of Central America. What reason will they have to complain, if we send among them our colonies, organized in this way with their sub-soil plows, their crow-bars, their hoes, their shovels, and their garden-seeds? What reason will they have to complain? Why, the fact is, that, unless our civilization is superior to theirs, the effort would, in the beginning, be a failure; it never can make one inch of progress. Then, sir, if we succeed at all, we succeed in planting a civilization there which is superior to theirs; we plant *that* or none. It is impossible for an inferior civilization to supplant a superior civilization except by violence, and it is almost impossible to do it in that way.

Well, sir, if we give them a better civilization, the tendency of that better civilization is to increase the value of real estate; for the value of property, the value of real estate, depends upon the character of the men who live upon the land, as well as upon the number of men who live upon it. Now, sir, we either make an absolute failure in this thing, and do not trouble them at all, or we give them a better civilization, and, in addition to that, we give them wealth.

Thus, sir, with bands of steel we bind the people of Central America to us and to our interests, by going among them in this way; and they cannot have reason to complain, nor will they complain. If we had approached them in this way two years ago, without this miserable meddlesome method, induced and warranted, or supposed to be warranted, by the neutrality laws, we would have filled Central America to overflowing by this time, and would have had with us the blessings of every native citizen in that portion of country.

Now, sir, if such is the way, if such is the power, if such is the effect of this method, to the emigrants, and to the people among whom they settle, why should we not now adopt it in reference to Central America? And what is the method? Why, it is as plain and simple as it can be. It is just to form a moneyed corporation which shall have two hundred thousand dollars capital; which shall then obtain and spread information through the country, by publications, indicating what are the natural resources of Central America, and the inducements to emigrate thither; showing how it is situated in relation to commerce, and how, of necessity, there must speedily be built upon that soil a flourishing Commonwealth. Then you have to apply a portion of these means to buying land and to sending out steam engines, and to building some hotels to accommodate the people who go there, and also some receiving houses for the emigrants. Establish there, and encourage there the establishment of the mechanic arts, and I tell you that every steam engine you send there will be the seat of a flourishing town: every one will be an argument for people to go there; for they talk louder than individuals a thousand times, and they are more convincing a thousand times, especially to an ig-

norant and degraded people, than any thing men can say, because the argument is addressed to the senses; it makes them feel comfortable; it gives them good clothes; it gives them money. These are the arguments to address to an ignorant and degraded people, and not cannon balls, or rifle balls, nor yet mere abstract dogmas about liberty or theology. Then let this company be organized as soon as you fix these neutrality laws so that we can get off without these vexatious executive interferences. [Laughter.] Then we shall see how the thing will work in Central America.

But, sir, I expect, when the people of the North shall hear that I am taking this view of the question, that the timid will be intensely terrified, and say that we are to have more slave States annexed to the Union. I have not the slightest apprehension of that result. It may be said that Yankees, when they get down into Central America, will, if the climate is suited for it, make use of slave labor. I have heard that argument before; and it has been asserted that the Yankees who go into slave States oftentimes turn slaveholders, and outdo the Southern men themselves. I have no doubt that they outdo them, if they do any thing in that line at all. [Laughter.] The Yankee has never become a slaveholder unless he has been forced to it by the social relations of the slave State where he lived; and the Yankee who has become a slaveholder, has, every day of his life thereafter, felt in his very bones the bad economy of the system. It could not be otherwise. Talk about our Yankees, who go to Central America, becoming slaveholders! Why, sir, we can buy a negro power, in a steam engine, for ten dollars [laughter], and we can clothe and feed that power for one year for five dollars [renewed laughter]; and are we the men to give $1000 for an African slave, and $150 a year to feed and clothe him?

No, sir. Setting aside the arguments about sentimentality and about philanthropy on this question, setting aside all poetry and fiction, he comes right down to the practical question—is it profitable? The Yankee replies, "not at all." Then there is no danger of men who go from Boston to Central America ever owning slaves, unless they are compelled to by their social relations there. If a man goes from Boston into Louisiana, and nobody will speak to him unless he has a slave, nobody will invite him to a social entertainment unless he owns a negro; and if he cannot get a wife unless he has a negro; then, sir, very likely he may make up his mind to own a negro. [Laughter.] But I tell you that he will repent of it every day while he has him. He cannot whistle "Yankee Doodle" with the same relish as before. He cannot whittle in the same free and easy manner. He used to cut with the grain, with the knife-edge from him; now, he cuts across the grain with the knife-edge towards him. The doleful fact that he owns a negro, is a tax upon every pulsation of his heart. Poor man! There is no inducement for the Yankees to spread slavery in Central America, and there is no power in any other part of the country to do it. Therefore, most fearlessly do I advocate the Americanizing of Central America. We must have some outlet for our overwhelming population. Necessity knows no law; and if we cannot have Central America, we must have the Indian Territory; we must have something; we are not exhausted in our power of emigration; we are worse off than we were before the opening of Kanzas. Not one-half of our natural increase has been exhausted in colonizing that Territory, and furnishing people for Oregon and Washington. We might, as I told you, make eight States a year, if we only used our forces economically; and we will use them economically by establishing, not for the present time only, but for all coming time, this system of organized emigration. Just as fast as this has become understood in the country — just as far as it is known to the people — not a single man who has any sense will emigrate in any other way than by colonies. Just look at the difference between men going in a colony and going alone. Suppose a man goes to Central America, and settles there alone; what is his influence upon real estate by settling there alone? There is no appreciable difference from what it was before; but if he goes there with five hundred men from the city of Boston to establish a town, by that very act he has made himself wealthy. I can point to numerous examples of the kind. Hence this making money by organized emigration is not going to be speedily relinquished. Depend upon it that we have only begun to use it, and that we have not used it with the efficiency with which it will be used in a year to come.

Now, sir, for these reasons I hope that the committee to which this question shall be referred, will so modify and elucidate the neutrality laws, that we shall not hereafter be subjected to this executive interference. And, in accordance with the views I have expressed, I now offer the following amendment:

"And, also, that said committee report, so far as they may be able, the present social and political condition of the people of Nicaragua, and whether they invite colonies from the United States to settle among them; and, also, whether the soil, climate, and other natural advantages of that country are such as to encourage emigration thither from the Northern States of this Confederacy."

Now, Mr. Chairman, I will state briefly my reasons for submitting that amendment. The gentleman from Mississippi (Mr. Quitman), referred to the social and political condition of the people of Central America, as a proper basis, I think he said, for our action. Therefore, with open arms, do we welcome that gentleman and his associates to our noble brotherhood of missionary political regenerators. For myself, I am willing to take the gentleman's words about the necessity of something being done to aid these people; but in grave matters of legislation like this, the committee having the subject in charge should first fully investigate in reference to the matter suggested by my amendment.

I do not intend any offensive sectionalism by using the word Northern; that the committee should inquire whether the natural advantages of soil and climate of Central America were such as to invite emigration thither from the Northern States. I so phrased the amendment because, as I have shown you, the Northern States are the only ones which can furnish emigration that would be of any consequence to Central America. We would be glad to receive whatever help the States on the Gulf could give us, but it is impossible for them to give much help in this work. And because the Northern States have the power in this matter, and because the Southern States have not the power, I have used the words, that the committee shall inquire specially whether the climate and the soil are such as to encourage emigration to Central America from the Northern States. If, however, there be objection to it, I will strike out the word "Northern," and leave the inquiry to be general.

A more withering reply was never made to the filibusteros of the country. This speech met them on their own ground, where they never expected to be reached. They thought of the populous North, pouring forth its surplus population after an organized system, and they trembled for their chances. Where numbers conquer, they know they must go down before them. Mr. Thayer's peculiar *manner*, too, told as effectively as his *matter*. The Representatives' Hall was alive all the while with laughter. But the hand-writing which this single speech served to bring out upon the wall read thus: EMIGRATION. The speaker stood forth the acknowledged apostle of "Manifest Destiny." He preached only the Civilization of Labor.

On the 25th of March, 1858, Mr. Thayer delivered another speech on the floor, entitled, "The Suicide of Slavery;" full of the same characteristics as his previous speech, but more compact and solid, more thoroughly considered, and requiring, from the nature of the theme, a strain of philosophic reflection in its treatment, yet it flashed with bright streaks of sarcasm, was alive with humor, and challenged serious attention on all sides. It was a capital effort, and developed the Emigration theory in a way likely to make a permanent impression. But the passage relative to the South as a Church, and what it had been doing for the Africans, is one of the finest pieces of satire we ever met with in our reading of oratory. Theodore Parker said of it, — "John Quincy Adams used satire in his way, and that, too, quite powerfully; but his satire was quantitatively great,— Mr. Thayer's is qualitatively nice and fine. There is no reply to such things. The account of the trials, dangers, and sufferings of the South to convert the heathen, is masterly; it is worthy of Dean Swift, but it is finer and subtler than any thing I remember from him."

The following is the speech itself:—

It may be expected, Mr. Chairman, that at this time I should say something in defence of the Pilgrims, and of the State of Massachusetts; for they have been repeatedly assailed on this floor, within the last two weeks. But I shall make no defence. There are some things which I never attempt to defend. Among these are the Falls of Niagara, the White Mountains of New Hampshire, the Atlantic Ocean, Plymouth Rock, Bunker Hill, and the history of Massachusetts. Any man may assail either or all of them with perfect impunity, so far as I am concerned. And words of disparagement or vituperation directed against either of these objects, by any assailant, excite in me feelings very different from those of indignation — whether the assailant comes with a bow as long as that of the bold Robin Hood, or with a bow of *shorter* range, like that of the gentleman from Alabama [Mr. Shorter] [Laughter.] But I deprecate the disposition that impels these shafts against the sister States of this confederacy. I deprecate this sectional animosity whenever and wherever I see it evinced. I have heard too much of the aggression of the North and of the aggressions of the South, in the past, to be very much in love with either of these ideas. I have never been accustomed to speak of the aggressions of the slave power, and I have no purpose of doing it now or hereafter. If the one-hundreth part of the people of this country can make dangerous aggressions on the rights and interests of the other ninety-nine hundredth parts of the people, either by the force of strength or by the arts of diplomacy, I assure you that I will be the last man to complain of it. I think that this slavery question is altogether too small a question to disturb so great a people as inhabit the United States of America.

For myself, I was always in favor of popular sovereignty, rightly so called. I am ready, for one, to agree to-day that the Territories belonging to this Government shall be open to settlement at any time, when Congress thinks fit so to open them, and that the people of all parts of the country shall go into them, with the assurance of *absolute and complete non-intervention;* with the assurance that whenever any chief executive, official, or non-resident, shall interfere, by fraud or violence, in their affairs, he shall either be impeached or hanged; with the assurance that when the people shall have the ratio of representation required by law, and shall come to Congress with a Constitution, republican in form, they shall be admitted into the

Union as a State. This, sir, is popular sovereignty, and it is what was practised in this country two centuries ago.

The people of the Plymouth colony had the privilege of choosing their own Governor, and of making their own laws. The same was true of the New Haven colony, and of the colony of the Providence Plantations. They alway did it. I believe the Crown of England never appointed a Governor for these colonies; certainly not for the last two. But were those people, without ever having exercised the right of self-government, better prepared to govern themselves than are our people, educated under our State Governments, who go into our territories? Why, then, should we continue to have an "Ahab to trouble Israel," while he lays the blame of his own misconduct upon the emigrant aid societies? Why not cut off these Territories from all connection with the General Government, legislative or executive? Then we shall have no more agitation in Congress, and no more contention in the Territories. But so long as this connection continues, so long as we have a President trying to bias by his appointments, and, perhaps, by the United States troops, the will of the people so long shall we have agitation, and we shall have enough of it.

Well, sir, I have nothing to find fault about. I am very well pleased with the present tendency of events. But, sir, there are those who are dissatisfied, and who are inclined to invoke a certain deity — I think a false deity —which presides over a portion of this Union; a deity which has been invoked by great men on great occasions, and by little men on little occasions, for a long time past — a deity in whose expected presence both the people and the politicians have sometimes stood aghast— "when he," in prospect only, "from his horrid hair shook pestilence and war." This sulphurous god is Disunion. This Capitol Hill has been a veritable Mount Carmel for the last quarter of a century, upon which experiments have been tried with this bogus deity. *One day* upon Mount Carmel was sufficient to determine the destiny of Baal and his prophets. But here, we, the most patient people in the world, witness these invocations *year after year*, with exemplary endurance, expecting that the great Is-to-be will some time come. And you and I, Mr. Chairman, even during the present session of Congress, have witnessed attempts to kindle here the fires upon the altar of Southern rights. But the sacrifice, the altar, and the spectators, were as cold as alabaster. The prophets only were warm; but they were warm, not from the presence of the god, but from his absence. He does not make his appearance. The great Is-to-be does not come. He has either gone on a very long journey, or else he is in a very deep sleep.

Well, sir, shall we have this deity of Disunion invoked forever? Who is to blame? If the North has given cause, what have we done? What cause of disunion has ever proceeded from us? Have you not had every thing your own way? Have we not let you have the Democratic party to use as you please? [Laughter.] Have you not had the Government for a long time? And have we not let you use it just as you had a mind to? We, sir, were busy about our commerce, extending it around the world; about our railroads; our internal improvements; our colleges, and all those things which interest our people. We knew that you had a taste for governing, and that by the indulgence you might be gratified without serious injury to us. For many years you have had your own way, but now you come here and cry out "disunion." Why, what more *can* we do?

Well, it may be that we have encouraged a mistake on your part. It may be that we have given you some reason to suppose that this temporary courtesy of governing, which we have extended, was a permanent right. However, if you have fallen into that error, we will, perhaps, at some future time disabuse and correct you. But whatever blame there is anywhere, whatever cause there is for disunion, must attach to the action of the slave power, commanding and controlling the Democratic party, and to no one else in the country. Therefore, at this time, I come with exultation—not, to be sure, with malignant exultation—to speak for a few moments upon the decline and fall of Slavery—nay, sir, further, upon the *suicide* of Slavery in this land. I will show you by what acts the two most important pillars of its support have been removed, and that the whole system of Slavery must therefore fall. And these two events have been accomplished, if not by its direct efforts, at least by the connivance of this same party, impelled by this same controlling agency.

I will first show you how the moral power of this institution has been destroyed, by what act, and then I will show you how and by what act its political power is forever doomed. But, sir, how did an institution like this ever have a moral power? is a question for us to examine. In the first place, we are told by Southern men that we have a nation of heathen in our land; and we are told by the same authority that we have an institution here for their regeneration. Now, sir, if we have, from necessity, a nation of heathen in our land, and if Slavery is an institution for their regeneration, it is very clear that Slavery has a moral power. But, says the gentleman from Georgia [Mr. Gartrell], speaking of negroes, "They are idle, dissolute, improvident, lazy, unthrifty, who think not of to-morrow, who provide but scantily for to-day."

I will also give you other proof. Here it is : —

" Who would credit it, that in these years of benevolent and successful missionary effort in this Christian Republic, there are over two millions of human beings *in the condition of heathen*, and, in some respects, in a worse condition ?. From long-continued and close observation, we believe their moral and religious condition is such that they may justly be regarded as the heathen of this Christian country."—*Committee of Synod of South Carolina and Georgia, in 1833.*

" After making all reasonable allowances, our colored population can be considered, at the best, but *semi-heathens.*" — *Kentucky Union's Circular to the Ministers of the Gospel in Kentucky, 1834.*

" There seems to be an almost entire absence of moral principle among the mass of our colored population."—*C. W. Gooch, Esq., Prize Essay on Agriculture in Virginia.*

" There needs no stronger illustration of the doctrine of depravity than the state of human nature on plantations in general. * * * Their advance in years is but a progression to the higher grades of iniquity."—*Hon. C. C. Pinckney, Address before the South Carolina Agricultural Society, at Charleston, 1829, second edition, pages* 10, 12.

The Maryville (Tennessee) *Intelligencer* of Oct. 4, 1835, says of the slaves of the Southwest, that their " condition, through time, will be second only to that of the wretched creatures in hell."

Here, then, is a field for great missionary labor; and it is fortunate that, under these circumstances, we happen to have an institution which is perfectly adapted to the regeneration of a lost and ruined race. I quote from the honorable member from the State of Virginia, in a speech delivered here, some time ago, in the House of Representatives :

" I believe that the institution of Slavery is a noble one; that it is necessary for the good, the well-being, of the negro race.. Looking to history, I go further, and I say, in the presence of this assembly, and under all the imposing circumstances surrounding me, that I believe it is God's institution. Yes, sir, if there is any thing in the action of the great Author of us all ; if there is any thing in the conduct of His chosen people; if there is any thing in the conduct of Christ himself, who came upon this earth, and yielded up His life as a sacrifice, that all through His death might live ; if there is any thing in the conduct of His Apostles, who inculcated obedience on the part of slaves towards their masters as a Christian duty, then we must believe that the institution is from God."— *Hon. Wm. Smith, of Virginia, in a speech in the House of Representatives.*

Again, I quote from the speech of the honorable gentleman from Georgia [Mr. Gartrell], in regard to this same sentiment :

" Every sentiment expressed in that eloquent extract meets my hearty approbation. As a Christian man, believing in the teachings of Holy Writ, I am here to-day before a Christian nation to re-affirm and re-announce the conclusion to which that distinguished gentleman came — that this institution, however much it may have been reviled, is of God."

Mr. Chairman, these are not the only authorities on this subject. You and I have heard from the other side, day after day, quotations from the Bible, intending to prove the same thing; and you and I know that there are honest men in the slave States who believe that this is a fact. I have seen such men myself, and have conversed with them. They have told me that Slavery was an absolute curse; and that the only reason why they held their slaves a day was, that they owed them certain religious duties, and must keep them to look after their spiritual welfare. They feared that if their slaves were cast loose upon the world, with nobody to look

2

after their spiritual interests, they would be spiritually lost. I heard this from a gentleman from Kentucky, and again from a gentleman from Augusta, Georgia, and I believe in my heart that both of these gentlemen were honest in these views.

I am not here to impugn any man's motives. I put this upon the ground that is claimed by Southern men; and when I listened to the gentlemen on the other side, reading honestly from the sacred volume in defence of this institution, as coming from God, and as a means for the regeneration of a heathen race in our land, I felt impelled to use the language of the Apostle to the Gentiles, which he employed on Mars Hill: "Oh! Athenians, I perceive that in all things ye are exceedingly given to religion." [Laughter.] Now, sir, since this institution has done all it ever can in this capacity, and since it is now destroyed as a converting and regenerating power, I stand here to give it its proper place in ecclesiastical history, for its right place it has never yet had.

In order to understand what position it is entitled to, we must, to some extent, speak by comparison, because we cannot speak absolutely on these matters of religion. The religious journals of the free States have oftentimes most unreasonably exulted over our religious efforts, when they contrasted them with the efforts of our Southern brethren. I have seen placed in parallel columns, in Northern journals, the contributions of the free States and the contributions of the slave States; and there were mighty words of exultation, unbecoming a Christian journal or Christian people at any time, when it was shown that our contributions for foreign missions were a hundred-fold more than yours. It is true we make more contributions. The city of Boston gives, for foreign missions, perhaps more than all the slave States; and the city of New York perhaps more than Boston. But what of that? We give a few cents apiece, and only a few cents, for foreign missions each year, which amounts to a great sum, because we are a great people. We send men to heathen nations far over the water, to tell them about their future destiny. We are careful not to send our *best* men; we keep our Notts and Waylands, and our Beechers and Cheevers, at home; but sometimes a Judson escapes from us before we know what

he is. This is about the extent we submit to self-sacrifice for the sake of the heathen.

Is there any cause for exultation in this, when we see what our Southern brethren have done and are doing? When have we ever taken the heathen to our hearth-stones and to our bosoms? When have we ever admitted the heathen to social communion with ourselves and our children? When have we ever taken the heathen to our large cities to show them the works of art, or to the watering places to show them fashionable society and beautiful scenery? Did you ever see a Yankee at the White Sulphur Springs shedding a benign religious influence over a little congregation of heathen companions? [Laughter.] We have pious women in the Northern States, whose bright example has made attractive the paths of virtue and religion. Conspicuous among them, in every good work, are the wives of our ministers and deacons; but not one of these, within the range of my acquaintance, would consider herself qualified, either by nature or by grace, to be chambermaid, dry-nurse, and spiritual adviser, to ten or twenty heathens in her own family. But, sir, had these worthy dames been *noble* dames; had they come down to us from the blood of the Norman Kings, through the bounding pulses of sundry cavaliers, and then had been willing to assume these humble offices of Christian charity, we should have believed the time, so often prayed for, had already come, when "kings should be fathers and queens nursing mothers in the church." Where, then, is the ground for this exultation on the part of the North? I tell you that it cannot be prompted by any thing but a rotund, bulbous, self-righteousness. So much, then, for the social sacrifices of our Southern brethren.

What other sacrifices have they made to regenerate this race? Great moral and intellectual sacrifices. I will read what Southern men say on this subject:

Judge Tucker, of Virginia, said in 1801:

"I say nothing of the baneful effects of Slavery on our moral character, because you know I have long been sensible of this point."

The Presbyterian Synod of South Carolina and Georgia said, in their report of 1834:

"Those only who have the management of these servants know what the hardening effect of it is upon their own feelings towards them."

Judge Summers, of Virginia, said, in a speech in 1832, in almost the same words:

"A slave population produces the most pernicious effect upon the manners, habits, and character, of those among whom it exists."

Judge Nichols, of Kentucky, in a speech in 1837, said:

"The deliberate convictions of my most matured consideration are, that the institution of slavery is a most serious injury to the habits, manners, and morals, of our white population; that it leads to sloth, indolence, dissipation, and vice."

So said Mr. Jefferson:

"The man must be a prodigy who can retain his manners and morals uncontaminated" [in the midst of slavery].

John Randolph on the floor of Congress, said:

"Where are the trophies of this infernal traffic? The handcuffs, the manacle, the blood-stained cowhide! What man is worse received in society for being a hard master? Who denies the hand of sister or daughter to such monsters?"

I might quote a hundred other Southern authorities of the same kind, showing the baneful effect of this institution upon the moral and intellectual character of the South. I might also quote from the United States census. I have the papers here, but time will not allow.

Now, in addition to these moral and intellectual sacrifices which our Southern brethren admit, there are pecuniary sacrifices which you know to be very great; indeed, had Virginia been free fifty years ago, had she been exempt from this great tendency to christianize the African race, she would have been worth more this day than all the Atlantic States south of New Jersey. And should she by any chance become free, you will see her wealth and her population increase in proportion as this missionary spirit is diminished. [Laughter.] It is true, our Southern brethren, impressed with this great idea of christianizing the African race, having for their only ambition to present the souls of their negroes, without spot or blemish, before the throne of the Eternal, have sacrificed almost every thing. I could quote from Southern men upon this subject. The sagacious states-

man who governs the Old Dominion, in a speech a few years ago, said:

"But in all the four cardinal resources — wonderful to tell, disagreeable to tell, shameful to announce — but one source of all four, in time past, has been employed to produce wealth. We have had no work in manufacturing, and commerce has spread its wings and flown from us, and agriculture has only skimmed the surface of mother earth. Three out of the four cardinal virtues have been idle; our young men, over their cigars and toddy, have been talking politics, and the negroes have been left to themselves, until we have all grown poor together."

But trials, and tribulations, and poverty, have ever beset the pathway of the saints. In the earliest days, they "wandered about in sheep-skins and goat-skins, persecuted, afflicted, tormented." Even now, in the nineteenth century, the condition of our Southern brethren is not much improved, since they are compelled "to chase the stump-tailed steer over sedge patches which outshine the sun, to get a tough steak," and to listen to the perpetual cry of "debts! debts!" "taxes! taxes!"

In this age of material progress, you have seen the North outstrip you; but, with true Christian patience and Christian devotion, you have adhered to the great work of regenerating the heathen. [Laughter.] Through evil report and through good report, reproached and maligned abroad by those who did not understand your motives, and, worst of all, sometimes abused at home by the ungrateful objects of your Christian charity, you have still pressed on towards the mark of your high calling. Now, sir, when was there ever a class of men so devoted and so self-sacrificing? I have read the history of the Apostles; I have read the history of the Reformers, of the Scotch Covenanters. of the Huguenots, and of the Crusaders; and, I tell you, not in one or all of these have I seen any such heroic self-sacrifice for the good of another race, or for the good of other men, as I do see in the history of these slave States. I have seen Fox's Book of Martyrs, but there is nothing in that to compare at all with the martyrs of the South. The census of the United States is the greatest book of martyrs ever printed. [Laughter.] Other books treat of martyrs as individuals; the census of the United States treats of them by counties and by States. I can see how a man, impressed with a grand and noble sentiment, should perhaps, in excitement or in an emergency, give up his life in support of it; but cannot see how a man can sacrifice his friends, his family, and his country, for a religious idea or an abstraction.

Here, then, sir, is the position of our Southern brethren upon this subject. But the worst is yet to be told—the doleful conclusion of the whole matter. They have made sacrifices, and it seems to me that they were entitled to the rewards for them; and I doubt not that they have often consoled themselves in contemplating the rewards in the future which must await them for such good services in the present. I have no doubt, sir, that oftentimes, seeing they have not treasures laid up on earth, they *supposed* they had treasures laid up in heaven. [Laughter.] But just at that time, when they seemed to be almost in the fruition of their labors, when the gentleman from Missouri [Mr. Anderson], in great exultation of spirit, was speaking of the institution that had raised the negro from barbarism to Christianity and civilization, and when the gentleman from Indiana [Mr. Hughes] had caught the inspiration, and said, that although the body of the African might be toiling under the lash, "his *soul* was free, and could converse on the sublimest principles of science and philosophy"—when faith had almost become sight—just then, sir, out comes the Supreme Court with the decision that A NEGRO HAS NO SOUL! [Laughter.] "Angels and ministers of grace defend us!" All these treasures that were supposed to have been laid up "where neither moth nor rust doth corrupt, and where thieves do not break through nor steal," have been invaded by the decision of the Supreme Court, and scattered to the four winds of heaven. More than two centuries of prayers and tears, of heroic self-sacrifice and Christian devotion, of faith and hope, of temporal and spiritual agony, have come to this "lame and impotent conclusion." [Laughter.] The moral dignity of the grandest missionary enterprise of this age is annihilated.

As a Northern man, I stand here a disinterested spectator of these events. If I do not like the decision of the court, I have a higher law. The negro himself can appeal to the court of heaven; but what refuge has the Southern church? [Renewed laughter.] None whatever. This decision is a blow, direct and terrible, falling with crushing violence upon our Southern brethren. This Supreme Court, with cruel and relentless hostility, has persecuted the Southern church as the dragon of the Apocalypse pursued the woman into the wilderness, seeking to devour her offspring. [Much laughter.]

What motives could have impelled the court to this act? I have no doubt a patriotic motive. I am not here to impugn the motives of any man, or of any set of men, much less of the highest judicial tribunal in this land. No doubt, sir, their motives were patriotic, for they had witnessed the devastation of this terrible religious fanaticism through the South. They had seen the ravages of this disastrous missionary monomania, and they determined that there must be an end of it; and how could they so effectually end it as by annihilating at once the object of its aims and aspirations. That, sir, they have done.

Here, then, endeth the *moral power* of the institution of Slavery.

I come now to the consideration of the event which just as surely has doomed to destruction the *political power* of that institution —I mean the repeal of the Missouri Compromise measure in the passage of the Kansas-Nebraska bill. That act, sir, I will show to you — if it ever was committed by the slave power — to have been a suicidal act. What need was there for repealing that Compromise, or of admitting Slavery into Kansas *by law?* Was not the South sure enough of the Territory as it was before? I think — and this is my honest conviction — that had it not been for that act, Kansas would have been inevitably a slave State. We of the North had no particular interest in that Territory. It was put down in our geographies as the great American desert. We had not considered it of much importance; but we relied on the *law* to keep Slavery out of it, and to preserve it to Freedom. We of the North have had too high an idea of the power of the General Government and of *law*, either *for* Freedom or *against* Freedom. Sir, this General Government has but little power over this question. It is not a *motive power*. It is only a *registry*, an exponent of power. It is the log-book of the ship of State, and not the steam engine that propels the ship, or the wind that fills the canvas. We would like to have the log-book kept right, to show us our true position; but we do not now consider the Government as the motive power. The motive power of this nation, as of all nations, is the people in their homes; and as the people in their homes are, so is your character and so is your progress. If the people in their homes in Kansas had been Pro-Slavery, what could the North have opposed to it? It was emigration, and emigration only, that could have made Kansas a State, either slave or free. The great law that governs emigration is this; that emigration follows the parallels of latitude westward. Under that law, Kansas would have been settled entirely by a Pro-Slavery people, as was the southern part of Indiana, and as was the southern part of Illinois. We in the North, trusting in the protection of the law, would have had no remedy. People in favor of Slavery would have gone there, and if they were compelled at first to adopt a free Constitution in order to shape their institutions according to any law concerning the Territory, they might have soon reversed that position. In fact, the decision of the Supreme Court has now made any such thing unnecessary. They might have formed just such a Constitution as they pleased. Well, then, we would thus, in all probability have had Kansas a slave State without the Kansas-Nebraska bill. But the passage of that bill, if Slavery had been certain before, *seemed* to the majority of the people in the North to make it almost inevitable. History warranted this fear. Judging from the case of Indiana, there seemed to be no chance whatever for Freedom in Kansas, after the opportunity for Slavery to enter there had been given. There was Missouri on the confines of the Territory — and the most densely peopled portion of Missouri, too. Freedom-loving men, desiring to go to that Territory, would have had to travel hundreds and thousands of miles. The men who lived on the line of Kansas, as well as other Southern men who entertained the same idea — though they did not express it then, for fear of losing the bill — anticipated that the passage of the bill would settle the question for Slavery in Kansas forever. That was the evidence of the early history of Indiana. When that Territory was opened for settlement, a few slaveholders, perhaps a dozen or a score, went over from Kentucky, and, con-

trary to the wishes both of the President and Congress, contrary to the ordinance of 1787, established Slavery; and they obtained such control over that young Territory, that petitions, signed by many of the inhabitants, praying Congress to suspend the prohibition of Slavery, were presented to Congress, year after year, from 1803 to 1807. These few slaveholders of the Territory of Indiana acquired such control over the inhabitants of that Territory, because they were an organization, as Slavery is everywhere and at all times an organization. It was a concentration of capital, a concentration of influence, and a concentration of power, which our emigrants from the free States, coming one by one, were unable to resist; and had it not been for the overwhelming population which poured in from the North in 1807 and 1808, the prohibition of Slavery would have been suspended. Had it not been for John Randolph, it would have been suspended in 1803; and had it not been for Mr. Franklin in the Senate, it might have been suspended in 1807; and both of these were Southern men.

Well, sir, I have said that slaveholders are everywhere an organization. There is a community of interest, a bond of feeling and of sympathy, which combines and concentrates all efforts to defend Slavery where it is, and to extend it to places where it is not. I will quote from the last number of *De Bow's Review*, everywhere acknowledged to be good Southern authority. In an article defending the New England Emigrant Aid Company, the writer says:

"We of the South have been practising 'Organized Emigration' for a century, and hence have outstripped the North in the acquisition of land. The owner of a hundred slaves, who, with his overseer, moves to the West, carries out a self-supporting, self-insuring, well-organized community. This is the sort of 'Organized Emigration' which experience shows suits the South and the negro race, whilst Mr. Thayer's is equally well adapted to the whites."

Then, what fault can be found with our efforts to organize Freedom by means of our emigrant aid societies, that enable our citizens to go to the Territories in companies of twenty, fifty, one hundred, or two hundred, to take possession of the West, and to locate there the institutions under which they choose to live?

And here I come to the defence of this association. It has been assailed, time and again, on this floor, and I have never been allowed even the privilege of putting questions to its assailants. The gentleman from Missouri (Mr. Anderson) called it "illegal and unconstitutional." It has been so assailed by the successor of Millard Fillmore. But where is the proof? Which of its acts has been shown to be illegal or unconstitutional? If it was illegal and unconstitutional, why has not the organization been crushed by the courts? We contend that any organization which is allowed to continue its existence from year to year, and to carry on its business, has the presumption, at least, of a legal right to do so. We claim that for the Emigrant Aid Company.

But the gentleman from Missouri professes to have authority in regard to this matter. He has said that we *may* employ this emigrant aid society in promoting emigration to Central America and to foreign countries, but that we must "*beware*" how we do so in colonizing the Territories of this Government. Mr. Chairman, if the gentleman from Missouri has any authority in these premises, I hope he will exercise it. I ask him to publish a hand-book for emigrants, telling us *how* we may go into a Territory; whether we *may* ride or *must* go on foot; whether we *may* take our wives and children with us, or *must* leave them at home; whether we *may* take some of our neighbors with us, with their agricultural implements and steam engines, or whether we *must* go into the Territories without any neighbors whatever; whether we *may* get horses or oxen from the free States, or whether we *must* content ourselves to take mules from the State of Missouri. [Laughter.]

Now, sir, let us have not only the book, but the reasons for it. Let us know how far we may go, according to the law, in this matter of emigration. I recommend the gentleman from Missouri to take some lessons from the gentleman from Mississippi, (Mr. Quitman), on the rights of emigration. I think he can get broader views upon this subject, if he will consult that gentleman, and I think he will allow northern men to go to the places which they have a right to go to by the law of this land, in such society, if it be law-abiding, as they may choose to select for themselves.

I have said that the great general law of emigration is, that the emigrants shall follow the parallels of latitude in this country. There are some exceptions to this. The gold in California led our emigrants from the extreme North across many parallels of latitude. That was a sufficient disturbing cause. The existence of Slavery in the slave States of this country has driven thirty-five out of every hundred emigrants across northern parallels to the free States of the Union. That was another great and powerful cause. But there is another cause sufficient to carry emigration southward over parallels of latitude. That is, the argument of cheap lands, with the additional advantage of organized emigration. The objections that have heretofore existed among Northern men to settling in Southern States are, by this mode of emigrating, entirely obviated. The Northern man, with his family of children, would not heretofore go into a Southern State, in the absence of schools and churches. But when combined with one or two hundred, or one or two thousand, of his friends and neighbors, he goes into a slave State, he carries with him schools and churches, and the mechanic arts, all these difficulties are obviated; and, besides, he has the inducement of going where the land can be bought at slave State prices, in the expectation of finding it come up probably in a few years to free-State prices, which are five or six times greater than slave-State prices. Here is the great inducement of increasing wealth. Let a colony start from Massachusetts, and settle on almost any land in the State of Virginia—in Greenville, Southampton, Dinwiddie, or Accomac, where the lands do not average so high as three dollars an acre, by the census of 1850 — and the very day they settle there, the value of the land is more than doubled. There is better land for sale to-day in Tennessee and North Carolina, for fifty cents per acre, than can be bought for ten times that sum in any free State.

How can such an appeal to the imigrating population of the North, in favor of organized emigration to the slave States, be resisted? I know of no means of resisting it. Certainly *you* can have no reason for resisting it, but every reason to encourage it. We do not come as your enemies; we come as your friends. We do not come to violate your laws, but to improve our own condition. This movement southward is destined to continue and to increase. Sir, if Slavery were as sacred as the Ark of the Covenant, and if it were defended by angels, I doubt whether it could withstand the progress of this age and the money-making tendencies of the Yankee. But it is *not* as sacred as the Ark of the Covenant, and nobody believes that it is defended by angels.

But, sir, there begins to be an enligatened idea in these border slave States upon this subject. A year ago, when I proposed to plant a few colonies in Virginia, several journals in the Old Dominion threatened me with hemp and grape-vine if I should ever set foot in that Territory. Well, I thought I would make the experiment. I went into western Virginia and into eastern Kentucky. I addressed numerous audiences in both of those States, and everywhere where I asked the people if they had any objection to their land being worth four or five times what it was, they said " No." [Laughter.] I asked them if they had any objection to the manufacture of ploughs and wagons in Wayne county. There never had been a manufacturing establishment between the Big Sandy and Guyandot. Though no portion of this continent is better situated for manufacturing purposes, having more than thirty thousand miles of river communication, which affords cheap transportation to the best markets, with a healthy climate and inexhaustible supplies of coal and iron and timber of the best quality. Yet every manufactured article was imported into this Natural Paradise of mechanics. There was not a newspaper published between the two rivers. I asked if they had any objection to a good, substantial, business newspaper published there, and to have schools and churches and the mechanic arts established in that county. With one voice they replied, " None, whatever." " We welcome you to our county, and to all its advantages." This was a generous and manly reception, worthy of the history of the Old Dominion. At every meeting we were welcomed by the unanimous voice of the people ; and now I believe that there are at least twelve newspapers in the State of Virginia advocating these colonies coming into the State. The sagacious statesman who is the Governor of the Old Dominion gives us a general and most cordial welcome. Well, the prospect is very good and inviting ; and if there is any danger of a dissolution of the Union — in fact, if there is any weak spot in the Union, I think it would be a good thing to patch it over with an additional layer of population. [Applause.] There never would be any disunion, if we could only attend to it, and see where the weak places are. and mend them in time.

But there is another exception to the rule I have laid down. Central America will prove abundantly sufficient to carry emigration southward, even across many parallels of latitude. She offers the grand inducements of commerce, of a climate unsurpassed in salubrity (in the central and Pacific portions) of a fertile soil, which yields three crops a year, and, more than all, lands so cheap that every man may buy. We have already begun to move, and what to some men seemed to be the unbilical cord of an embryo Southern Empire, is likely, by these means, to be cut off, if it is not cut off already. [Laughter.] Everybody knows the physiological consequences.

Well, sir, I wish now to say that there is a higher power than man's in relation to this matter of Freedom in Kansas. It seemed at first to the whole North that the project of establishing Slavery there would exclude Freedom, and the whole North was intimidated by it. There was the greatest reluctance manifested to emigration in that direction from the North. Everywhere there was fear ; everywhere despair.

> There was silence deep as death,
>   While we floated on our path ;
>   And the boldest held his breath
>   For a time."

Six months of persistent effort in writing and speaking were required to induce the first colony of only thirty men to go to Kansas. The people had become impressed with the idea that Kansas was destined to be a slave State ; but as soon as the first colony had reached that Territory, and had founded the famous city of Lawrence, the whole train of Northern emigration was turned from Nebraska and from Minnesota to Kansas. And they have filled Kansas with Free State men — such men as are fitted for the high position they occupy ; for Kansas is the geographical centre of our possessions. Its position in itself makes it the arbiter of our fate in all coming time, destined to give law to all between the Missouri river and the golden gates of the Pacific, and to make its power felt all the way between the British possessions and the Gulf of Mexico. Never were more noble men needed for a more noble work. It was necessary that Plymouth Rock should repeat itself in Kansas. The Puritan character was needed there; but how could it be had, except by such discipline as made the Puritans; for if it was necessary that they should be elevated like the Pilgrim Fathers of New England, it was also necessary that they should have the training of the Pilgrim Fathers. They were peculiar in their early history, and peculiar in their late history. They had their early education among the rocks and mountains of New England. I have known of great men in times past, who came from the forest, who came from hills and mountains; but I never have known them to be raised on Wilton carpets. These men received their early training among the rugged hills of New England, where they waged incessant war on ice and granite, on snow and gravelstones. It is there where they acquire their energy and their power. And, sir, I think the Yankee race has at least an octave more compass than any other nation on earth. I *know* a Yankee doughface is half an octave meaner that any other man. [Laughter.]

Sir, some of the best of this Yankee race went to Kansas. They were stigmatized, six months before they arrived there, as thieves and paupers. Well, if such men as those who have built Lawrence, and Topeka, and Manhatten, and Ossawatomie, and Quindaro, were thieves and paupers, what do you think we respectable, well-to-do people, will accomplish in the Old Dominion, where we are now becoming acquainted with some of the "first families?" These Free State men of Kansas have been reviled by their inferiors at both ends of Pennsylvania avenue many times during the last three years. The other day, in the other end of this Capitol, such men were denominated *slaves*. Sir, we are slaves! I, admit it; *but our only master is the Great Jehovah.* These heroes in Kansas having for their ancestors the Pilgrim Fathers, "sons of sires who baffled crowned and mitred tyranny," disciplined in their early years by the rugged teachings of adversity, seem to have been well prepared for their high mission.

But the discipline of worthy example, of New England education, and of poverty and adversity were not enough. The discipline of *tyranny* was requisite for their perfection. This discipline has been of use in all ages of the world. David was not fit to rule over Israel until he had been hunted like a "partridge in the mountains" by the envious and malignant Saul. Brutus was not fitted to expel the Tarquins until he had endured their tyranny for years. What would Moses have done, but for Pharaoh? Where would have been the Reformers of the sixteenth century, where the Puritans in the seventeenth, and the Patriots in the eighteenth, but for Leo the Tenth, Charles the First, and George the Third? But Charles the First lost his head, and George the Third his colonies, for less tyranny than has been practised upon the people of Kansas by the two successors of Millard Fillmore. If we thank God for patriots, we should also thank Him for tyrants; for what great achievements have patriots ever made, without the stimulus of tyranny? Without vice, virtue itself must be insipid; and without wicked and mean men, there could be no heroes.

The brave man rejoices in the opposition of the enemy of his rights. Wicked and mean men are the stepping-stones on which the good and great ascend to heaven and immortal fame.

These miscreants, cursed both by God and man, subserve important interests. The sacred volume which unfolds to us the life and sufferings of the Saviour of men, makes record also of Pontius Pilate and of Judas Iscariot as necessary agencies in that great redemption.

So I will denounce no man who has fought against Freedom in Kansas, as entirely useless in the grand result. But what a team to draw the chariots of freedom! Atchison and Stringfellow and John Calhoun, with the two successors of Millard Fillmore to lift at the wheels.

———

In the autumn of 1858, Mr. Thayer was a second time nominated for Congress. He appeared before the convention that nominated him, and addressed them on his position and views. The result was, that he was endorsed with great enthusiasm, both by the convention and his constituents. He was returned to Congress by an overwhelming majority, the best proof of the esteem in which his services and character were held at home.

He delivered a third speech in Congress, on the 11th of February, 1859, on the admission of Oregon; a speech that made a great deal of talk in the Republican party, especially as, by the aid of a few Republicans, Oregon was finally admitted as a State. With the promulgation of this liberal and statesmanlike speech, which was characterized by all of its author's usual energy, clearness, and practical force, was opened upon him an opposition by a portion of the press of his own party, that has not ceased till the present time. It is against these very assaults that he is defending himself to-day. Oregon was admitted by the votes of eleven Republicans in the House of Representatives, Eli Thayer leading the column.

The speech is as follows:—

Mr. Speaker : My colleague [Mr. Dawes] who has just addressed the House is unable to see how an honest Representative of the State of Massachusetts can vote for the admission of Oregon. Well, in the exercise of charity, I can see how a Massachusetts Representative, both honest and patriotic, can vote *against* the admission of Oregon. He can do it by not comprehending the question, or he may do it in obedience to party dictation. I will now show my colleague how an honest Representative can vote *for* the admission, if he will listen to my argument and the reasons which I shall give in defence of my position.

Mr. Speaker, I think this is a strange necessity that compels the Northern Representatives upon this floor to give the reasons for their votes for the admission of another free State into this Confederacy. Sir, I shall vote for the admission of the State of Oregon without hesitation, without reluctance, and without reserve. So far as my vote and my voice can go, I would extend to her such a welcome as becomes her history, as becomes her promise for the future, and such as becomes our own high renown for justice and magnanimity — a welcome not based on contemptible political calculation, or still more contemptible partisan expediency; but such a welcome as sympathy and friendship and patriotism should extend to another new State; such, sir, as becomes the birthday of a nation.

This people comes before us in accordance with the forms of law, and upon the invitation of this House; and it is too late to apply a party test upon this question. On the 19th of May last, a vote was taken in the Senate upon the admission of Oregon, and eleven Republican Senators voted for her admission, while six Republican Senators only voted against her admission; and, sir, I have not heard of any attempt, on the part of the six Senators who voted for the rejection of Oregon, to read out of the Republican party the eleven Senators who voted for her admission; and if that attempt is now to be made, we will see whether it is in the power of a minority of the people to read a majority out of the party.

But, sir, who are these people of Oregon, who come here now, asking admission ? They are the pilgrims of the Pacific coast. If they are fanatics upon some subjects, we can refer to the pilgrims of the Atlantic coast, who also were fanatics upon some subjects. But, sir, if the pilgrims of the Atlantic coast finally became examples to the world in all that exalts our race, may we not hope that the pilgrims of the Pacific coast may yet become worthy of our esteem?

Nearly one-quarter of a century ago, in my boyhood, I studied the adventures of those men, who founded upon the western shore of the American continent what are now the cities of Oregon and Astoria. These men, who were then in the vigor of their lives, are now old men — gray-haired and trembling with age. Their work of life is nearly completed; and this day they are sitting by their hearthstones, waiting to know what is to be the result of our deliberation; waiting to know whether the proud consummation to which they have aspired for the last twenty years is now reached; and whether Oregon, which, in toil and trial, in defiance of danger and of death, and with persistence and endurance such as belong only to our race, they have brought to her present proud and prosperous condition, is now to be placed upon an equality with the original States of this Confederacy.

These are the men who have carried our institutions to the remotest boundaries of our Republic. These are the veterans of the art of peace. American valor with conquering arms has carried our flag by Monterey and

Chepultepec until it was planted upon the halls of the Montezumas. But far beyond those halls have these heroes borne the victorious arts of peace. In the Territory of Oregon they have established our free institutions. There, sir, strong and deep, they have laid the foundations of a free State, and they come here, like the wise men of the East, not *asking* gifts, but *bringing* gifts; in that respect unlike our military men, who expect and receive honors and rewards for their services. What do they bring? Why, sir, the trophies of their own labor, the evidences of their own worth. They present before us the cities and towns which they have founded. They present schools, churches, and workshops. They bring all, all the products of their labor, and place them upon the altar of the Union, a pledge for the common welfare and the common defence. And what are we doing here? Why, sir, quibbling about things which are comparatively unessential, and which pertain exclusively to the people of Oregon, and not to us or our duties here; quibbling about points which, if New York or Massachusetts were in the place of Oregon, would secure some votes on this side of the House against their admission. Massachusetts, which you know, sir, I never defend anywhere, even Massachusetts does not allow the negro to be enrolled in the militia of the State. These, then, are the men who come here; and what if they have some ideas and sentiments with which we do not agree—is that a reason why we should excommunicate them; that we should have nothing hereafter to do with them?

What law of reformation is this? It is the pharisaical law of distance, distrust, and derision. It is not the Christian law of contact, confidence, and communion. The Pharisees denounced the Founder of Christianity as "the friend of publicans and sinners." That class would repel all who do not agree with them to the fullest extent. Shall we pursue a similar course in relation to the people of Oregon? Is it wise to do so? Is it expedient to reject their application on such grounds?

What objections do Republicans present to this application? They say there is not sufficient population, and they claim that it is their mission to see that the Democratic party shall recover its consistency. At whose expense? At the expense of the consistency of the Republican party. I submit that it is better for the Republican party to preserve for itself the consistency which it possesses, rather than attempt to recover for the Democrats the consistency which they have lost.

Then, sir, in relation to this qualification of population, what is the position of the Republican party, and what has it been? This party by its Representatives, voted for the admission of Kansas under the Topeka Constitution, with less than one-half of the present population of Oregon. The Republican party in the House, without one exception, so far as I know, voted for the enabling act, inviting Oregon to come here, with a Constitution, to be admitted as a State. I have no disposition, and there is no need, to inquire here what is the population of Oregon; for, as a Republican, I am pledged to no rule on this subject. I opposed, as did my colleague, and my friends on this side of the House, the restriction which was put upon the Territory of Kansas. We protested against it then, and protest against it now. We have no sympathy whatever with that restriction, and are ready, at any time, to give an honest vote for its repeal.

Another objection is urged against the clause in the Constitution of Oregon which excludes negroes and mulattoes from that Territory; and, in addition, provides that they shall not bring any suit therein. It is said that this is in contravention of the Constitution of the United States. This I do not admit. But what if it is? The Constitution presented by the people of Oregon is not submitted to our vote. We cannot amend it; all we have to do about it is to see that it is republican in form. If it is unconstitutional, it is not in the power of Congress to impart to it the least vitality, and it will fall by its own weight. But gentlemen argue here, as if we could by our votes give life and power to an instrument in violation of the Constitution of the United States. Sir, this argument is weak and futile. Congress itself derives its own vitality from the Constitution, and how can it impart a greater vital force than it has received? The stream cannot rise above its source.

But should the Constitution of Oregon be proved unconstitutional before the proper tribunal, then, sir, will it follow that we have violated our oaths, by admitting Oregon into the Union with that organic law? By no means. We have not sworn that the people of Oregon shall support the Constitution of the United States. We have sworn to support it ourselves, not that anybody else shall do so.

But, sir, this provision is no more hostile to the United States Constitution than are the laws of Indiana and Illinois which exclude free negroes and mulattoes from their boundaries. Certainly not. It is no more to exclude the suit of the man than to exclude the man himself. Is the negro less than his suit? I contend that he is greater than his suit. The greater contains the less, and the statutes of Illinois and Indiana are as unconstitutional as is the provision of the Oregon Constitution. But it does seem, at the first view, that it was a wanton and unprovoked outrage upon the rights of these men who are excluded from that State. I think there is a real apology for the action of the States of Illinois and Indiana. They are in close proximity to the institution of Slavery. They are under the shadow of the dying tree of Slavery, and its decayed limbs are constantly threatening to fall upon their heads; and I cannot censure them for taking such means as they see fit to protect themselves from such imminent peril. I am not disposed to call into question the right or constitutionality of their action.

Is there *no apology*, then, for the people of Oregon? Have they committed a wanton and unprovoked outrage upon the rights of negroes and mulattoes, in excluding them from that Territory? I say that there *is* an apology, and that it consists in this: they believed that they were obliged to choose between a free-State Constitution with this provision, and a slave-State Constitution without it. There were three parties in the Territory at the time this Constitution was made and adopted. There was the Free-State party, which was composed of Free-State Democrats and Republicans. There was the Pro-Slavery party, in favor of a slave State. There was, between these two, a very considerable party, supposed to hold the balance of power, and that party I may characterize as the anti-negro party. They said that they would sooner vote for a slave State that for a free State with a Constitution admitting free negroes and mulattoes. They preferred to have slaves in Oregon rather than free negroes; and it was for the purpose of securing their vote for a free State that the Republicans and Free-State Democrats inserted and advocated this provision. The leading Republicans of that Territory advocated the adoption of the Constitution containing this provision. Mr. Logan, who received every Republican vote for United States Senator, advocated, on the stump, the adoption of the Constitution with this clause.

What was the vote? Why, sir, this clause of the Constitution had a majority of seven thousand five hundred and fifty-nine votes; while the Constitution itself had a majority of only four thousand votes. The Democratic majority in the Territory, as shown in the election of a Representative to this House, was only one thousand six hundred and thirteen votes. Then it is proved, by the official record, that the Republican party combined with the Free State Democratic party to sanction and ratify this provision of the Constitution which is here called in question. There is also abundant evidence, outside of the record, to satisfy any one that such is the fact. This, then, is the apology for the action of the people of Oregon on this question. What Republican, or what friend of free States, is justified, under these circumstances, in voting to exclude the people of Oregon from this Confederacy on account of this provision, which is only an expedient, and not a thing for practical use? It is very easy, at this distance, to censure the people of Oregon, and to pronounce judgment against them; but such judgment may be neither wise nor just.

> " Then at the balance let's be mute,
> We never can adjust it ;
> What's done we partly may compute,
> But know not what's resisted."

But, sir, there is another objection urged from certain quarters, with great pertinacity. I mean the objection to the suffrage of aliens. The Constitution of Oregon, in respect to alien suffrage, is certainly more stringent than the law of some of the States of the Union, and less stringent than that of others. It is the same as the Territorial law has been during the last ten years. It requires a residence of twelve months in the United States, and of six months in Oregon. It requires that the sworn declaration of an intention to become a citizen of the United States shall have been on file at least one year. What was the inducement for that encouragement of aliens? The wages of labor are now, and have been, in Oregon, double what they are on the Atlantic coast; and I ask, would it be expedient or wise for Oregon to drive away from her borders the emigration from Europe, on which she has to rely for developing the resources of the country? Certainly not. Such a policy would have been disastrous in the extreme to the young State. It was wise and prudent, therefore, for Oregon to invite and encourage that emigration which she so much needs, to develop her great resources, and to secure for her the products of her natural wealth.

These, sir, are among the plausible and ostensible objections that have been urged on this side of the House against the admission of Oregon. There is yet another argument; that Kansas has been excluded from the Union by the action of the Democratic party; and that, therefore, Republicans ought to exclude Oregon. The argument amounts to this: that we should abuse Oregon because the Democratic party have abused Kansas. Now I, for one, am quite content that the record of the Republicans, in respect to Oregon, should be better than the record of the Democratic party in respect to Kansas. I am quite content that the record of the Democratic party, in respect to Kansas, should be just what it is; and I do not think it is possible very much to improve the Republican record, or to impair the Democratic record. Are we to sacrifice our own political principles and advantages, for the sake of compelling the Democratic party to consistency of action? Are we bound, as a party, to sacrifice our own consistency in doing so? Certainly not. I think the Republican party has another, and, to my mind, a less difficult mission to perform; and that is, to preserve its own consistency.

These are some of the palpable objections that have been urged on this floor. I come now to some for which I thank the gentleman from Indiana [Mr. Hughes]. He has presented to the House some *secret* objections which the Republicans are said to have to the admission of Oregon. The first is, that the Republicans are opposed to the admission of Oregon, because it is a Democratic State. Now, sir, does not the gentleman from Indiana understand that the Republican party is not so devoid of sagacity as to fail to see that to reject a young State for the reason that it is Democratic would make

it Democratic forever? Does the gentleman from Indiana find any thing in the history of the Republican party which justifies such conviction of its stupidity, as would lead him to say that the Republican party, as a party, is opposed to the admission of a free State because her people had chosen such politics as seem to them best? Does he not see that sagacious Republicans, finding that the Republican party in Oregon is now in a minority of only a few hundred votes, understand that if Oregon be admitted by their action, and were thus set free from the influence of Executive patronage, she would very soon become a Republican State?

But further than that: the gentleman brings up another secret reason why the Republicans would oppose the admission of Oregon. That secret reason is, that, in case of the failure of the people to elect a President, and in case of that election coming to this House, there will be a vote from Oregon against the Republican candidate, which may procure his defeat. Now, does not the gentleman from Indiana understand that any such position of the Republican party would secure its defeat? that if it were stupid enough to take a position against the admission of free States, because their Constitutions were not universally approved, it would require more than the vote of one State, either in Congress or out of Congress, to help or harm the prospects of the party? I thank the gentleman from Indiana for the secret reasons which he has given, which I have thus far been enabled to prove too absurd and impolitic to influence the action of the Republican party.

There are certain principles which, in my opinion, should govern the House on a question of the admission of a State. First, the Constitution must be republican in form. Second, there must be sufficient population; what number may be sufficient, must be left to the discretion of Congress. Third, the proposed admission must be shown to be for the benefit of the contracting parties; to be best for the State applying, to be best for the Confederacy. Let us look at these principles, and see how they should affect the vote on the admission of Oregon. First, then, is the Constitution presented by Oregon republican in form?

I will here send to the Clerk's desk a quotation from an authority which is justly and generally respected by Republicans — an extract from a speech of Senator Seward, made in the Senate of the United States last May, upon this very question.

The Clerk read as follows :

" I think there is nobody who doubts that the people of Oregon are to-day ready, desirous, willing, to come in. They have made a Constitution which is acceptable to themselves, and a Constitution which, however it may be criticised here, after all, complies substantially with every requirement which the Congress of the United States, or any considerable portion of either House of Congress, has ever insisted on in regard to any State.

" It seems to me, therefore, to be trifling with the State of Oregon, trifling with the people of that community, and to be unnecessary, and calculated to produce an unfavorable impression on the public mind, in regard to the consistency of the policy which we pursue in admitting States into the Union, to delay or deny this application. For one, sir, I think that the sooner a Territory emerges from its provincial condition, the better; the sooner the people are left to manage their own affairs, and are admitted to participation in the responsibilities of the Government, the stronger and the more vigorous the States which those people form will be. I trust, therefore, that the question will be taken, and that the State may be admitted without further delay."

Mr. Thayer. So much, then, in relation to the first principle which should govern our action in the admission of States. And what, sir, concerning the other? How will it affect this present Confederacy of States, to admit the Territory of Oregon? Why, gentlemen talk here as if we were discussing the question of admitting some new and unheard-of race of monsters and cannibals into the Union! Sir, is not this injustice to the people of Oregon? Will they contaminate this Confederacy? Just as much as their mountain streams will contaminate the Pacific ocean. I tell you, they may be inferior to us in education, in refinement, and in etiquette; they may not appear as well in the drawing-room as some of our Eastern exquisites; but in the sturdy virtues of honesty, of fidelity, of industry, and of endurance, they are above the average of the people of this Confederacy. I regret that the gentleman from Maine (Mr. Washburn) the other day deemed it expedient to call the pioneers of our national progress, "interlopers, runaways, and outlaws." I affirm, concerning American citizens in any Territory of the United States, and in any new State of this Confederacy, that they are above the average of the population of the old States, in all that makes up manly and virtuous character. They have my sympathy; and never will I oppress them by my vote or my voice.

But, sir, what if the people of Oregon were really as bad as the most unfavorable construction of their Constitution, and the speech of my colleague (Mr. Dawes) would represent them to be, then what should we gain by refusing them admission into the Union? If the objectionable features in their Constitution are their true sentiments, and are placed in the organic law for use, and not for expediency, then surely the evil is deeper than the ink and parchment of their Constitution. It is in the hearts of the people and will not be eradicated by any harsh treatment that gentlemen on this floor may recommend. I doubt whether you will effect the salvation of the people of Oregon by heaping curses on their heads, or by excluding them for unworthiness. You may send them away from the door of the Capitol, but they will go thinking less of you, and less subject thereafter to your influence. They may come again with a hypocritical Constitution, trusting to effect by statute law what you would not allow in organic law. They may not come at all, or they may come with a Constitution tolerating Slavery. Discouraged and repulsed by Northern votes — finding no sympathy where they had most right to expect it, they might not be able longer to resist the Slave-State party in the Territory, acting under the Dred Scott decision. Is it not right, therefore, for the lovers of Freedom to advocate the immediate transition of Oregon from the condition of a Territory in which Slavery is lawful, to the condition of a State in which it is forbidden? Which do we choose, a *slave Territory* or a FREE STATE?

But, sir, there is another argument which may influence some members who doubt the security of this Union of States. By this act which I now advocate, we shall bind firmly to the old States, by indissoluble bonds, the remotest portions of our possessions. This will make secure all intermediate parts of the national domain.

This, then, may be grateful assurance to such as want assurance about the permanency of the Union. For myself, I have not much respect for any such assurance; but I do have an utter contempt for any doubts on the subject. This Union, Mr. Speaker, is not a thing to be argued for and advocated; it is a thing settled, fixed, and determined. Far transcending in importance the temporary convenience of any one State or of all the States, it is in our hands, a trust, not for our posterity only, but for the world. We are bound to deliver it unimpaired to succeeding generations, and we WILL so deliver it. THE UNION IS AND WILL BE.

If, then, there is a great gain to the Confederacy, is it not also better for the people of Oregon themselves that she should be admitted into the Union? Is it better that they should remain under the tuition of this Federal Government — a non-resident Government — or that they should govern themselves? Why, sir, to contend against the advantages of self-government would seem to me unsuited to this place, and not to comport well with the history of this Republic; for the origin of this nation was a protest against a non-resident Government, and our history should be. For one, sir, I have no faith in that kind of government being exercised over Anglo-Saxons anywhere, and least of all have I faith in that kind of government being exercised by Republics anywhere; and, therefore, to relieve a portion of our people from what I consider a curse—the curse of a non-resident domination — I will cheerfully vote for the admission of Oregon.

Sir, this non-resident control is a relic, as it was an invention, of ancient tyranny. It has come down from the history of the old Romans, who had pro-consuls in Judea, in Spain, in Gaul, in Germany, and in Britain; and England has copied their example, and sent Governors and Governor-Generals to India, and to this continent also. But we protested successfully against that kind of government by the war of the Revolution; and I look forward to the time when every portion of our national domain shall be free from it; when we shall have no provincial dependencies whatever; when we shall have nothing but a combination of equal and sovereign republics. Then, sir, we may bring the duties of this government to a position where they will be, as was well said last session by the gentleman from Alabama [Mr. Curry], "few and simple," as they should be.

It is in accordance with this view that I shall oppose any thing that leads to complications—that shall multiply or extend our provincial dependencies.

I shall oppose all protectorates over foreign countries; all military occupations and military usurpations; all annexation of territory, except as independent sovereignties acquired and at the same time admitted into the Union by treaty stipulations as States equal to any in this Confederacy. It will never do for us to imitate the despotisms of Europe. We must adhere to the original, simple plan of this Confederacy, which did not contemplate provincial dependencies, or armies and navies, necessary for their acquisition and control.

So far as we deviate from the simplicity of the plan of the fathers, just so far shall we advance towards danger, disaster, and destruction.

But, Mr. Chairman, I did wish to review the action of the minority of the Committee on Territories in relation to this question, but my time has nearly expired, and I can only refer to it.

They have reported the bill of the majority with an additional provision repealing the clause of the English bill restricting the right of Kansas to come into the Union with a less population than ninety-three thousand. Now, sir, I had supposed that the gentlemen of the minority of the committee would have voted for the bill which they have reported, but speeches have been made by two of the gentlemen who signed that report [Mr. Grow and Mr. Granger], in which they went off on an altogether different line of reasoning. They have talked about the unconstitutionality of the Constitution of Oregon, and about its invasions of human rights, without confining themselves at all to the argument of their minority report. They argue that whoever may vote for the admission of the State, will properly be held responsible for all these outrages. And now I wish to know for what consideration the signers of that report are willing to ignore all these revered human rights, invaded and ruined by the Constitution of Oregon? I have their reply in this report. On one condition they are willing to sanction all these outrages; and that condition is, that a certain act concerning Kansas shall be repealed. If the report is in good faith there can be no other conclusion.

On the 24th of the same month, he took occasion once more to assert his views in relation to the best mode of winning the Territories over to Freedom, which is simply by giving to Free Labor *fair play* in the struggle with Slave Labor. Hence the speech was itself entitled "Fair Play." It is one of the best of all his remarkable Congressional efforts. It is particularly happy as illustrating his *practical views* on the whole subject under discussion, — views that no abstract theorizing can hope to reach or overthrow. The reader will find, in its perusal, that he has come to know and admire the author of it more than ever. All the cavils of party presses at either its positions or arguments appear narrow and of no consequence, for *they* seem to be striving for mere partizan success, while *he* seems to be struggling only for permanent benefit and real truth. Here is the speech : —

Mr. CHAIRMAN : The gentleman from Maine [Mr. Washburn], in his speech the other day, recommended to the Republican party to "note the policy of the Democratic party, and to learn wisdom from their opponents." Advised by such high authority, and scorning no source of knowledge, however humble, I have for a few days made a study of the discipline and policy of the Democratic party; and what do I find ? A wonderful toleration of hostile and conflicting principles and measures, prompted by adverse and contending interests. I believe that the plain of Shinar never witnessed about the base of the tower of Babel any such confusion of languages as we see here of principles and measures in the Democratic party. How do they stand upon the tariff ? Some are for specific duties, some for *ad valorem* duties, and some for no duties at all. How concerning the Dred Scott decision, and the protection of slavery in the Territories ? Some are for the non-intervention of the federal government with slavery in the Territories, and some are for the direct establishment of slavery in the Territories by the federal power, as the journal of this House will show, by the notice which has been given of a bill to be introduced for the protection of slavery in the Territories, and as the debate in the Senate yesterday will show ; while others are in favor of making all such schemes of protection null and void by the unfriendly legislation, or by the masterly inactivity of the settlers. And how about the acquisition of territory ? Some are for acquiring it by fillibustering and the force of private crusades ; some by the more dignified method of protectorates, military occupations, and military usurpation ; some by purchase, and some by war. And how is it about the slave trade ? Some are for reviving it, and some are utterly hostile to its revival. And so in reference to the Pacific Railroad, and every other measure of public policy. I have said enough to show that there is a toleration in that party of the widest diversity of principles, opinions, and measures.

Now, sir, if I am to learn a lesson from this party, I think I may learn this lesson, — that while I would not tolerate any such latitude of opinion as would breed confusion in the Republican party, I would tolerate such liberality of sentiment as shall not compel men who agree in practice to quarrel about matters of faith. I do not advocate that proscriptive policy which would drive away from me men who do not agree with me about the importance or necessity or expediency of legislating against slavery, or for freedom in the Territories. While I will not denounce the gentleman from Maine, for his favorite measure, I shall expect the same toleration for my own. He may bow down in his chamber three times a day before the Wilmot proviso, with his windows open toward Jerusalem, and I will not trouble him for that. But when he attempts to fit other Republicans to his bedstead, we shall very likely protest against any such act, especially if it involves the necessity of cutting us off at both ends. I maintain my right to think well of Wilmot proviso men, and to think well if I choose of those who are not Wilmot proviso men. The Wilmot proviso is only a measure, not a principle.

Now, sir, there are some classes of men who profess to belong to the Republican party, to whom I do not propose to address any remarks upon this occasion, because I believe that, politically, they will not be made better and that they cannot be made worse.

I shall first speak of a class which I will denominate THE RIGIDLY RIGHTEOUS, who claim that it is not enough that a State shall exclude slavery from its limits, but that this act must proceed from most exemplary and Christian motives. The State must exclude slavery because it is a sin. It might as well be a slave State as a free State if it is not made free upon the purest Christian principles. These pinks of piety deprecate any appeal to national or personal interest; they deprecate any argument which is based upon œconomical or pecuniary consideration as an attempt to contaminate the purity of exalted anti-slavery sentiment, and to soil by earthly contact the pure and spotless anti-slavery standard of the North. With this class I can never agree, for I would rather see a State free for the worst reasons, than see it slave for the best reasons.

Another class consists of the PRE-EMINENTLY CONSISTENT. Some years ago they pointed their guns at the enemy; and they intend to fire where they first aimed, whether the enemy be there or not. [Laughter.] To-day you find them pouring their hot shot into the cold ashes of the enemy's extinct camp-fires. [Laughter.] And they say, "is it any reason because the enemy has changed his position, because *he* is unstable and inconsistent, that *we* should be wavering and inconsistent also ?' [Laughter.] With this class I do not agree. I am for pointing our guns where the enemy now is — for pointing them where the enemy stands at the instant when we apply the torch.

There is another class, sir, composed of the political Cassandras of the Republican party, who are always prophesying, in the middle of one great disaster, that another still greater is about to come — who are continually saying that slavery has always had its own way, and always will have it — that slavery, under the Dred Scott decision, will yet be established in Massachusetts and New Hampshire — that secret intrigues are going on for establishing it in Canada, as well as for putting the White Mountains and Cape Cod under the lash. [Laughter.] I have an account to settle with these men. I have met them, and found them a great impediment to the progress of freedom in this country. In the contest for free men and free labor in Kansas, I affirm here that they were a greater obstacle to our progress than the border ruffians, the cabinet and power of President Pierce, or the bad travelling in the State of

Missouri; for they were filling the country with the cry that Kansas was lost. With quivering lips and moist eyes they went about crying that *all was lost.* The effect was to send hundreds and thousands of men, who would have joined our good colonists in Kansas, shivering away to the cold regions of Minnesota. I have no sympathy with these men. Of this class was Uzza in the days of David, who thought that because the oxen stumbled, the ark of the Lord would surely fall; and he stretched out his trembling hand in support of Omnipotence. Smitten by the Power which his doubts had insulted, faithless Uzza died upon the spot. Why he died I ask no commentary to tell me. Why any such are left is not so clear. Without faith, either in the power of God or the destiny of man, they libel freedom and slander freemen. They have no joy in the present and no hope in the future. They seem predestined to disaster and defeat; and woe to the party or project in which they assume authority or exercise influence.

To a man of this class the present life is one perpetual nightmare; and what the future will be, who can say ? Can he be saved ? Can a man be saved without faith, or hope, or works, with only repentance — and even that consisting not in sorrow for his own sins, but for other people's virtues ? [Laughter.] Why, what if by some chance he were once in the Holy City ? — he would be no more *saved* than he was before. He never would see the tree of life or the river of life, never would have a harp in his hand — but a spyglass, and skulking about the battlements, and peering off into illimitable space [laughter]; if he should chance to see Dred Scott or the Supreme Court, even though they might be beyond the great gulf, he would think they were coming to establish slavery on the golden pavements of the New Jerusalem. [Laughter.]

Now, sir, I do not address myself to these men. They bear the same relation to the Republican party that Cape Fear and Cape Lookout do to this continent. They serve only to keep people away from it. [Much laughter.] I address the continent of the Republican party, and not these insignificant though conspicuous capes and promontories. And, in doing it, I shall refer to first principles. It is an axiom in physics that one body must sustain to another, one of three relations. It must be either less, equal, or greater; and it is in accordance with the law of growth that if one organized body is less than another, and, by natural and gradual accretions, shall at some time become greater, it must first become equal. Now, sir, in politics it is also an axiom that if one cause is inferior to another in position or in importance, it can never become superior except by first attaining to a position of equality. Now, sir, freedom and slavery are two causes in our politics, and it is claimed by gentlemen that the cause of freedom is in an inferior position politically (and this I assert too), and has been so for years. The question then is how it shall attain to an equal position, and, perhaps, hereafter to a superior position. It can only attain to that superior position in the legislation of this Government, and in the executive power of this Government, by first attaining to a position of equality. And it is this policy of striving for this position of equality that I have advocated for years; and I am rejoiced that at the present time I am sustained in this argument by very high authority. I find that one of the distinguished Senators from the State of New York [Mr. Seward] made a speech last November, in which he took this position. Part of that speech was made in Rochester, the other part of it was made a few days later in Rome.

The speech altogether contains two main propositions. The first proposition is this: that the Democratic party ought to be put out of power. The second proposition is the method by which this can be accomplished. Under the first head the speaker, not having much to prove, and therefore being free from the necessity of laborious concentration (because a Northern audience was willing to assent without argument) very naturally digressed from the strict line of logic, and discoursed freely upon a collateral philosophical question. He entered into a harmless philosophical speculation about the comparative vitality of free labor, and of slave labor, and I think he came to the conclusion that free labor has the greater vitality. This I consider a very harmless speculation; and had a similar one been indulged in, as it has often been, by a Southern statesman, and a contrary conclusion arrived at, no Northern man would have thought of taking exception to it. He might have concluded, as Mr. Fitzhugh has done in his Sociology, as Southern ora-

tors have often done on the stump, and as Southern editors have often done in their papers, that slave labor had the greater vitality, and would hereafter override free labor in the Northern States. Well, sir, so much for the very harmless speculation which has been very much misrepresented. But the sum total of the Senator's argument — the conclusion, which was . for immediate and practical use — was what may be considered a sound national platform for the party opposed to the Administration. It is broad enough for all the elements of the opposition to combine upon, and to occupy safely. Now, sir, what is that platform? What are the words of wisdom which give promise of victory? Here they are:

" The work of to-day is to obtain securities for fair play in this great contest. Fair play was all that was left to James Buchanan and his administration to afford us. He promised us that miserable right — the remnant of all other valuable rights. Even that promise was broken, and that right has been treacherously wrested from us the first year of the administration of James Buchanan. The President, without rebuke from Congress, and with the acquiescence of the Senate, successively removed Gov. Walker and Gov. Stanton, for yielding to the people of Kansas free, fair, and impartial elections. When the people of the State of Kansas by such elections repudiated the slavery Lecompton constitution, and avowed their · unalterable determination to remain a community of free men, the Congress of the United States remanded them to remain indefinitely a slave-holding Territory. · Elections for slavery are held valid and lawful ; elections for freedom are deemed invalid, idle, and futile. Have I not said truly, then, that our first conquest must be the recovery of fairness and equality between freedom and slavery in the conduct of the administration, and of legislation: at Washington."

" Fairness and equality between freedom and slavery in the conduct of the administration and in the legislation at Washington!" What, sir, is this but non-intervention by the federal government, either for freedom or slavery in the Territories ? What is this but a national platform upon which all the elements of opposition to the present administration can fairly stand? I subscribe to that doctrine, and advocate a fair play par—

ty, and a fair play President, upon a fair play platform; I am for fair play between section and section, between State and State; for fair play for our foreign policy, and for fair play for our domestic policy; for fair play with England, France and Spain; fair play with China and Africa; for the acquisition of Cuba, Central America, and Mexico, by fair play, and by that only. Here, then, is the position which the opposition can fairly assume, and the platform has the highest Republican authority. Sensible and practical men will harmoniously endorse it, and be proud to stand upon it and defend it in the next national campaign.

In relation to slavery in the Territories, and the connection of the federal government therewith, there are three political positions, and only three. First, there is intervention for slavery; second, there is intervention for freedom; and third, there is no intervention whatever. What is the present policy of the Democratic party in relation to this question? and what has been its past position? I say that party has been, as it is now, in favor of intervention for slavery. I say that while that party has advocated popular sovereignty, and has elected one President by that advocacy, it has always persistently voted against popular sovereignty. It voted against it in the spring of 1854, upon Senator Chase's amendment to the Kansas bill, giving to the people of Kansas and Nebraska the right to choose ther own officers. It was voted against when the Toombs bill was voted for by the Democratic party, imposing a constitution upon the people of Kansas without their approbation. It was voted against by the Democratic party when they voted for the Lecompton bill, which sought to impose upon the people of Kansas a constitution, not only without their approbation, but in defiance of their solemn protest. It was again voted against in rejecting the Crittenden-Montgomery amendment, which gave to the people of Kansas the opportunity of framing their own constitution — of choosing under what organic law they would live.

But, sir, while the Democratic party excluded Congress from intervention with slavery in Kansas and Nebraska, they did not exclude the President from interfering by the use of his patronage and power. The intervention of despotic unity was preferred to the intervention of Congress for the establishment of slavery in Kansas; and, sir, I think they had a tool at that time which was well adapted to the uses for which it was designed. It was supple, pliant, and fitted for many uses. Hudibras had such an instrument — his dagger.

"'Twould scrape trenches or chip bread,
  Toast cheese or bacon though it were
  To bait a mouse-trap would not care,
  'Twould make shoes clean, and in the earth
  Set leeks and onions and so forth."

So much for the past position of the Democratic party in relation to intervention in the Territories. Now, what is its present position? Is that party now upon the popular sovereignty platform? Did the debate in the Senate yesterday show that? Are they not in favor of intervention, and that of the fiercest kind, against freedom and for slavery in the Territories? And what does that notice mean upon your journal of a bill to be introduced which shall provide for the protection of slavery in the Territories? What mean those Southern journals when they demand that a federal law shall be made by Congress for the protection of slavery in the Territories? I refer, first, to the Charleston (S. C.) News, which says:

"If the constitution confers upon slavery the right to go to the Territories, as according to the Kansas Nebraska bill and the Dred Scott decision, it does, then it also imposes the duty of protecting that right, and this cannot be done without positive Pro-Slavery legislation and a Federal Slave Code for the Territories."

Again: The Richmond Enquirer says:

"The right of property in slaves in the States is now placed, practically as well as legally, beyond the reach of Federal legislative encroachment. But in the Territories the case is different. It is not sufficient that the decision of the Supreme Court prevents Congress and all its delegates from the prohibition of slavery in a Territory. There must be positive legislative enactment; a civil and criminal code for the protection of slave property in the Territories ought to be provided."

In the same spirit is the following extract from the New York Day-Book:

"Of course, the people of a Territory, when they frame their State constitution, may adopt or exclude slavery; but while they are a Territory, if they fail to protect property invested in the person or industrial capacity of a negro, they grossly violate equal rights, and therefore are not authorized to consider themselves Democrats. The whole question is resolved into this simple right or no right to protection to slave property in the Federal Territories, and, as the Charleston News suggests, it must constitute the issue of 1860."

We find such opinions becoming prevalent in the Democratic party, and it is demanded that they shall be made the test of party fealty. Then we must come to the conclusion that the Democratic party is to-day against popular sovereignty; that it is in favor of Federal intervention, of Executive intervention, legislative intervention, as well as a judicial intervention, for slavery in the Territories of the Union.

Well, sir, what is it proposed now to oppose to this pro-slavery intervention in the Territories? Is it said that we will oppose to it the Wilmot proviso? I respect the sincerity of those who recommend this as a panacea for all the evils that threaten our Territories, but I cannot highly esteem their intelligence if they believe it can be applied. For how many years is it since any party in Congress had the power to pass the Wilmot proviso in reference to the Territories? Quite a number. And how do the people of this country stand upon that question? In the last two Presidential contests they have repudiated that measure, and to-day we find the people against it, Congress against it, and we have it intimated to us that the Supreme Court would declare it unconstitutional. Then, under these embarrassments, shall we unavailingly strive to apply it until all the territory of the United States shall have been settled and its destiny sealed forever, either as slave or free. Then it is an impracticable and an antiquated issue, and sensible and practical men will now cease to urge it as a party policy. Such men now see that they could not apply any such prohibition if they would, and I hope they will not repudiate those who would not apply it if they could.

If then, as I have shown, there can be no Federal intervention for freedom in the Territories, we can only choose between intervention for slavery, and no intervention at all. Then, sir, without hesitation, while I deny no principle of the Republican party, I advocate the adoption of the policy of no more Federal intervention with respect to slavery in the Territories.

But what *really is the position* of the Republican party upon this question? Can you show an instance in our history in which we have gone against honest popular sovereignty in the Territories? What act in this House, or in the Senate, will show that the Republican party has been against popular sovereignty? During the contest in Kansas all we asked was that the people should be let alone, and that they should have the right to do as they pleased. We voted for the Chase amendment in 1854. And how did we vote last session upon the Crittenden-Montgomery bill? Every man upon this side of the House sustained it. Are we not then the party not only in favor, but also in possession of popular sovereignty? We have captured that gun before the enemy had even used it, and now we propose to test its range and accuracy by some experiments on the Democratic party.

But does any man say that he voted for the Crittenden-Montgomery bill in an emergency, and that he sacrificed his principles in doing it? I doubt whether this will be said. I did not sacrifice my principles by that vote; on the contrary, I voted in accordance with my principles. And, sir, I have but a poor respect for principles that will not do in an emergency, — that will not do in a storm. Such principles are not fit to keep in fair weather. Well, sir, that is the policy of the Republican party,—at least, it is the practice of the Republican party, and non-intervention is perfectly consistent, therefore, with its present principles. It is not only perfectly consistent for the party, but it is perfectly safe, as I will show you, for the cause of freedom. I can refer you to the history of Kansas. Kansas, without any protection for freedom, has become a free State, or at least she is this day prepared to be a free State, and will never be any thing less. In defiance of numerous obstacles in the way of obtaining her freedom, she has bravely secured it. In the immediate vicinity of the Platte purchase, the most intensely pro-slavery portion of Missouri, there, almost in the bosom of slave States, there, far removed from the States of the North, which furnish emigrants to the West, and with all the force of the General Government against freedom, and for slavery in the Territory, the free State heroes have triumphed; and not only that, but they have put forth many times the power which was requisite to accomplish the grand result. If it had not been for Executive intervention, and for the cowardly predictions of faint-hearted anti-slavery men in the North, that Kansas would be lost, I think, sir, that the contest might have been ended before the year 1856.

But as it was, notwithstanding all the obstacles in her way, the contest began to grow insipid during that year for want of opposition from the pro-slavery side, and I left it, as Atchison and Stringfellow had already done. Since that time we know very well what has been the history of Kansas. It is now apparent that there are at least eight or nine free State men in that Territory to one slave State man. Whatever may have been intended, such, sir, has been the effect of adopting this principle, which has compelled Northern men to rely upon themselves, and act upon their own responsibility in this matter of making free States. This is safer than to leave this question to Congress and to law. I have a thousand times more confidence in the people than I have in Congress on this subject.

Now, Mr. Chairman, compare the resources of these two causes that contend for pre-eminence in the Territories,—free labor and slave labor. How do we find the wealth and numbers of the North when contrasted with those of the South? I shall not dwell upon this point, for on a former occasion I opened that greatest book of martyrs, — the Census of the United States, — and showed how these facts were.

But how do the North and South compare in the power of combination? Why, we men of the North, called the Northern hive, live in towns and villages. Even our agricultural districts are quite densely peopled. We have, in Massachusetts, one hundred and thirty men to the square mile. If there is any difficulty abroad or at home, — if there is any need for immediate action or remote action, it is easy for us to assemble, and consult, and determine what action is needed, and what shall be most effective. And, sir, when it was necessary to put some colonies into Kansas, I found no difficulty in having meetings in these towns and villages at very short notice. Plans were formed for making colonies, and for taking possession of the country in dispute, and thus

the result contemplated was accomplished. But how can any such concert of action exist in that part of our country where there is only eighty-nine one-hundredths of a man to a square mile! What chance of holding meetings, of kindling enthusiasm, of taking council, and of laying plans for accomplishing grand results? None whatever.

Then, sir, added to this ready combination, we also have great facilities of locomotion. Our people can migrate with but little difficulty. If there were a meeting to-night to put a colony into Kansas, all the arrangement might be perfected, and complete preparation made for starting in two weeks. The next day after the meeting you would see flaming hand-bills on the streets headed, "Ho for Kansas!" "Property for Sale!" Daguerreotypes of some "familiar faces," and perhaps the old homestead, would be taken, and in two weeks the colony, on the lightning train, following a pillar of cloud by day, and a pillar of fire by night, would be going on its way to their prairie home.

How can a Southern planter hope to rival this speed and readiness of transition? After he has determined to emigrate, his plantation is to be sold, and the purchaser is to be hunted up, and much time is required. And after a purchaser is found, credit must be given of from one to twenty years. But suppose all this accomplished, and the whole train of servants made ready for the journey, how like a funeral procession would they appear loitering along through the swamps of Alabama and Mississippi. No, sir, you cannot compete with us in this game of emigration. We evidently have the advantage of you every way. You have not power to make a contest in this matter interesting. I say this in no spirit of malignant exultation. I am laying down facts, and I wish Southern men to understand their bearing and inevitable consequences.

But, sir, the Southern planter does not take his force of negroes to a disputed Territory. The case which I was just now supposing never really occurs in practice. It did not once occur during the contest for the Territory of Kansas. I have never heard of a single slaveholder who took there even as many as five negroes.

The spirit of devotion and the spirit of Christianity sometimes prompt to great sacrifices, but I am compelled to believe that the Southern planters are few in number who will hazard the loss of their slaves, even for the grand purpose of securing "scope and verge" to African Christianization.

If, then, there is no motive of Christianity potent enough to influence slaveholders to move with their slaves to the Territories of the West, there certainly can be no other sufficient inducement. There can be no pecuniary inducement to convey slaves where the very soil under their feet will be in dispute, and where the slaves themselves may be confiscated by an organic law excluding slavery from the new State, or by the statute law of the Territory, called "unfriendly legislation."

Again, sir, there is a converting power in these free State colonies, and it is a wonderful power. I assert, on the best authority, that the majority of the inhabitants of Kansas, who went there from slave States, are to-day free State men. They came in contact with these Northern communities, they learned some facts of which they were not before cognizant, and they made up their minds that it was best for them and their children that Kansas should be a free State. This converting influence extended to the Governors of the Territory. "The extinguishers themselves took fire," and to this day they give a charmingly brilliant light.

Now, sir, in addition to these resources, contrast the causes themselves, which are in conflict. Contrast free labor with slave labor. What are their histories and what their relative power? Free labor has covered the once sterile hills of New England with orchards and gardens and corn-fields. It has filled our valleys with the music of machinery and the hum of busy industry. The same creating power has built thriving cities and towns upon our western waters, and clothed the prairies with fields of waving grain. Scaling the Rocky Mountains, the same majestic power has opened the golden gates of the Pacific, and has transformed the solitary wilderness,

" Where rolled the Oregon, and heard no sound,
Save his own dashings,"

into a prosperous State, destined to become the most important seat of commerce and manufactures on our Western coast.

Here are some of the trophies of free labor. Others yet, and greater, will be secured in the future. Stronger than Briareus, and possessing more arms than the giant monster brought to defend the throne of Jupiter against assailing Titans, free labor, unaided by law, relying solely on its own inherent energy, will always be found able to protect its own inheritance.

But where are the triumphs of slave labor? I will not reply, — I press this comparison no further.

Now, sir, there is no chance of making another slave State from any Territory belonging to this Confederacy. I state this as a fair and well-founded conclusion, that it may be considered by men from all portions of the country. I think that sensible men from the South already consider it a settled fact. What need, then, of quarrelling about measures for securing what is already secure? Security is all we ask, and that we have. That is the grand result of a contest to which you invited us, and to which we reluctantly came. We did not propose to you this very unequal game of emigration. It was a game which was proposed by the Democratic party, and the South enlisted in it, under the lead of that party. And what was the stake? You compelled the North to stake Kansas on that game, while you voluntarily offered to stake all the other Territories. For one, I was ready to accept that challenge. I was ready to enter upon that game upon such terms. I did do it. I do not now regret it. I do not want it otherwise than it is; for all that we have lost in achieving the victory that we have gained is more than ten thousand times repaid in that disciplined army of freemen, who are determined to see that all is right, from Minnesota to the Gulf of Mexico. These are the facts, and it is better for the whole country that such are the facts.

There are two blunders that the South has made in following the lead of the Democratic party. The first is the blunder of the free trade policy, which has compelled us to leave our native homes and make free States in the West. We could not be idle, and when you would not let us make cloth in New England, we have gone about making States on the prairies. What, now, would have been the result, if an opposite policy had prevailed? What, if the South and the Democratic party had allowed abundant protection to our manufacturing industry? By that protection our manufactures in New England would have increased in nearly the same ratio as the production of cotton in the Southern States. That has been the fact essentially with the cotton manufactures of England. Why would it not have been so with our own, had they been sufficiently protected. But ours have remained almost stationary for the want of this protection. We have therefore gone about making markets for our future products, and in that we have done well. If our manufacturing industry had been protected as I suggested, New England would to-day have had double her present population, and I think that our free States would not have extended one whit beyond the Mississippi. I doubt whether they would have gone beyond Indiana. The South could have taken possession of the great West by that policy; she would have become the agricultural power of the Union emphatically. But now free labor has already taken possession of much, and, as I have shown, will yet take possession of the remainder of the public domain. The thing is inevitable. It must come. I do not stand here, as a New England man, to find fault with these results; whatever may be said about the motives which secured them, the results are good. We have secured for all future time, the best market in the world, and New England will yet see brighter and better days than she has ever yet seen. No portion of the country can ever compete with her in the manufacture of cloths, or of boots and shoes; no portion can ever compete with her in ship-building, or in the carrying trade of the Atlantic coast. She has now prepared for herself this extensive market of free States, which is every day increasing. The difference between a free State market and a slave State market is almost beyond calculation. It is a difference based both on the quantity and the quality of the goods which we manufacture, as well as on the security for pay. Who, then, can condemn us 'for having enlisted in this crusade for freedom in Kansas with so much zeal, when we understood that her freedom would inure to the benefit of New England industry hereafter forever?

Some men may have had a more exalted motive—no doubt many had—no doubt there was much of sentiment, and much of benevolence and Christianity also, in these efforts; but if there had been nothing but wise pecuniary forecast in them, even that would have been reason enough for our honest efforts to make free States. Here, then, we see that the free-trade policy of the slave States has effectually restricted slavery and extended freedom.

The second grand political blunder of the South, under the lead of the Democratic party, was the repeal of the Missouri Compromise. When you rested on the pledges of implied law, you were sure of securing for slavery a large portion of the public domain; but when, under the delusive hope of acquiring Kansas, you invited the North to contend with you in this game of emigration, you abandoned the last solitary hope of slavery extension on this continent. This Kansas contest has created more working anti-slavery than all other causes in our history. To be sure, we had some dreaming sentimentalists before, who felt enough, but who expended their feeling in harmless speeches and resolutions. There were, also, some political anti-slavery men, who relied on law and nothing else to restrict slavery and extend freedom. But the repeal of that compromise gave us free State settlers instead of free State sentiments. It made the people rely upon themselves rather than on law and politicians. It has given us a race of workers instead of a race of wishers; and now, whatever may come hereafter, we shall always remember that the surest defence of freedom is a guard of free men at the point of conflict. The history of that conflict has shown us that the extension of freedom has no necessary connection with the success of party politics; that the people, independent of political organizations, can make free States, even when the whole power of this government is exercised against them. Who, then, can for a moment doubt concerning the result when the people shall have fair play and non-intervention in the Territories by the Federal Government, instead of perpetual and persistent federal intervention for slavery?

These two comprehensive blunders of the South, under the Democratic party—the free trade policy and the emigration contest—induced by the repeal of the Missouri Compromise, have secured beyond question the freedom of every foot of the national domain. In commemoration of these transcendent Southern illusions, I think the abolitionists ought to erect one grand enduring monument.

How, then, can this policy of non-intervention in the Territories, which I have advocated, be embodied and made practical? There are two ways by which that may be accomplished. One way is, by allowing the people of the Territories to elect all their officers. I am utterly opposed to the organization of 'another Territory without such a provision in the organizing act. Another way is, to allow no more Territorial organization whatever. Some men may consider this as unsafe. I do not recommend it now as a policy. I *suggest* it as a policy to be considered, whether it might not be better hereafter, never, in any way, to increase our provincial dependencies. Such dependencies do not become this government. They are entirely hostile to the genius of republican institutions. There is nothing in the origin of this nation which should encourage this provincial system for our Territories. I would feel perfectly safe to allow our emigrants, with the Bible and the common law, with the axe and the plough, to go into the national domain and take care of themselves. How would such a policy affect the Treasury of the United States? It would save us millions of dollars annually. Our people would then go forward in solid phalanx. They would be able to protect themselves. There would be no deterioration in education or morals; for the settlers, living contiguous to each other, could support schools and churches. We would then have no difficulty whatever arising from Indian wars, and no difficulty arising from the numerous applications of Territorial office-seekers.

Sir, we have history on our side in favor of that policy. The people of Oregon governed themselves for ten years before the Congress of the United States extended their protecting hand over the colony. They had a perfect system of government—a perfect system for the administration of justice. They had a symmetrical and well-appointed government in all its branches. They established post offices and post roads. According to the testimony of the first Governor of that Territory, every thing was progressing with as much regularity and order and success as it could have been if it had been all planned by the powers in this city, and put in operation by their agents. But we have a present example. Dacotah is to-day without a Territorial government, and yet we hear of no disturbances there. The people have established a government for themselves, and I much doubt whether it is in the power of Congress to improve it by establishing, in its stead, a non-resident jurisdiction. But, sir, there are earlier examples of the successful working of this policy than are furnished by either Oregon or Dacotah. I refer to the early colonies of Plymouth, Providence, and New Haven, whose histories are household words.

Wherever you look, you find that our people, whether they be few or many, are abundantly able to take care of themselves. Therefore, I suggest, as a policy to be considered — whether there shall hereafter be another Territory organized in the national domain—whether we have not had sectional quarrels enough and difficulties enough about provincial dependencies, to induce us to create no more, and as speedily as possible to get rid of what we now have.

Now, sir, I have advocated an open field for a fair conflict between these two opposing systems of labor. If you, sir, claim that slave labor is a divine institution, I claim that free labor is a divine institution, and I, for one, am willing that hereafter the two institutions shall honestly contend and grapple, and that the stronger shall prevail, and I will acknowledge that the one which shall prove the stronger in a fair contest is the more divine.

Now, sir, in all that I have said upon this subject, I have nowhere denied the power of Congress to exclude slavery from the Territories. On the contrary, I believe that power is clearly established, not only by legal construction of the highest authority, but also by the authority of our history and practice. Still, sir, I should deem the exercise of that power inexpedient at the present time if it could be applied. Nothing should be attempted by law which can be accomplished without law. The extension and security of free labor cannot be effected by law, but by work. It would be a hazardous security for the North to rely on law to prohibit slavery in the Territories, when, she can so much more safely rely upon herself. But, sir, we have no power to prohibit it by law, and since we have not, I do not regret the fact; I say that I am willing that this conflict should go on, and that it should come to a decision which is based upon the merits of the contending systems, and upon nothing else. And the more cheerfully do I assent to this arrangement, because it will furnish a sound basis of legislation to ages yet to be. But if to-day slavery is obstructed by law, if to-day slavery is crushed out by the legal enactments of this General Government, and not by the laws of the communities in which it is practised, then what objection could be urged when a future generation, here or elsewhere, shall propose to establish slavery instead of free labor? Why, it would be said that slavery did not have a fair trial in the United States of America; that it was crushed by the opposing force of law; that it did not fall from its own inherent weakness and lack of vitality; and there might be force in that argument.

But, now, let the question be determined by the merits of the two contesting systems, and let the mighty and majestic power of free labor overthrow and destroy slave labor in a fair fight, as it surely will, then what will be the effect upon the future? Why, if any legislator shall then presume to suggest to this nation, or to any other, that slavery is better than freedom, and shall make an honest proposition that it be established, the student of history will meet him, and, turning back to the records of this contest, will show him the evidence of the invincible power of freedom, and of the inherent imbecility of slavery. He will trace the majestic progress of free labor all the way across this continent, from the granite hills of New England to the rocky ramparts of the Pacific. He will show that it was mightier than Presidents and Princes, Courts and Counsellors, Cabinets and Congresses. While slavery, nurtured and caressed by the whole power of this confederacy, appeared but a dwarfed and impotent cripple, in this contest with the heaven-born giant. Then, sir, ages hence, when the actors in these present scenes shall have been forgotten, should it be proposed again to establish slavery, in this or in any other land, the people will ponder upon the progress and the grand result of this last great battle between these hostile powers, and will proclaim with one voice that freedom, having fairly conquered, shall evermore remain in possession of the field, and of the well-earned laurels of victory.

The vexed Utah question was on the carpet during the next session of Congress, and Mr. Thayer gave expression to his views on POLYGAMY, on the 3d of April, of the present year. His individuality of thought is plainly stamped on the speech, and his genius for solving knotty problems in politics in a practical way is brought into the foreground more than ever. The army had been tried in Utah, but to no purpose; the topic only returned upon Congress to haunt it with a consciousness of its own inefficiency. In this dilemma, the plan suggested by Mr. Thayer was hailed as an ingenious one, certainly a' a peaceable one, and, what is best of all, as a perfectly *practical* one. Not all legislators can say this of their suggestions. His plan was for a reconstruction of the old territorial boundaries, so as to divide up Utah between the population at Pike's Peak, and that in Carson Valley; and thus *the people themselves*, rather than Congress, would dispose of the evil of polygamy on the spot. The simple proposition shows its author to be of a statesmanlike turn, and a man to be looked to in any public emergency.

Said Mr. THAYER — Mr. Speaker, it has become apparent, in the progress of this debate, that there is at ‾least one question on which the representatives of all portions of the country may agree. Every member from every section of the Union is ready to assert the odious criminality of polygamy. It is encouraging, it is refreshing, to know that there is at least one subject on which there is no sectionalism, in relation to which we have not heard the Representatives of North Carolina boasting that their people are much better than those of Massachusetts, nor the Representatives of the State of New York boasting that their people are better than those of Mississippi.

There is really, now, one practical question before us for our decision; and, sir, in my remarks upon it, I shall not treat it as an abstraction. I shall not treat it as a figure of speech, nor as a legal technicality. Polygamy is an existing fact; and as an existing fact, while I agree with members from every part of the country in denouncing it, will so act as to insure its most speedy extermination. Is this a fact, sir, which began to-day, or yesterday, or last week? I should suppose, from the zeal which is manifested here, that it never was heard of till the beginning of this session of Congress.

But, sir, some thirteen years ago, one Brigham Young, a shrewd and selfish and unscrupulous adventurer, led certain Mormons from Illinois, or from Missouri, across what was then called the great American desert, by a long and wearisome journey, to the basin of the Great Salt Lake. Poor, deluded, ignorant fanatics were his followers, who, from having no religion at all, had been captivated by the theories of Joe Smith, and had joined the ranks of the Latter Day Saints. From time to time, there have been accessions to their number. Year after year, they have come from Wales and Scotland, from England and Germany, and from the States of this Confederacy. About two years ago, they attained their highest power. They are now declining in strength, harmony, and consolidation, and are diminishing in numbers. As a separate and peculiar community, they are doomed to speedy extinction. Congress has endured their increasing strength, and the insolence of their highest power, without action. Can we not possibly endure their decline and extermination, without this exhibition of paper authority and of spasmodic morality?

In the course of these thirteen years of Mormon history, we have had a Whig Administration, we have had two Democratic Administrations, and at one time, for one Congress, the Republicans had the organization of this House; and sir, there never has been an act passed against this crime, to make it a penal offence. There it was, before the eyes of the country, before the world, and before Congress; but still no party, until this day, has taken the responsibility of proposing that it should be abolished by penal statute and by force of arms. Now there seems, as I said before, to be a feeling in this House, not known in the community at all, which could be accounted for only on the supposition that polygamy never was heard of till to-day. There is a spasm, sir, of morality, or a paroxysm, or a panic, or something that seems to impel certain men to feel the necessity of voting, and of voting now, against polygamy, at all hazards.

Mr. REAGAN. I desire to correct the gentleman on a point of fact. He is mistaken in supposing that nothing has ever been done upon this subject. I introduced a resolution during the last Congress, which was adopted by the House, referring the subject to the Judiciary Committee for inquiry.

Mr. THAYER. I said no act had been passed. That was my assertion. And now, sir, there is most intense zeal manifested that something shall be voted — voted, not done — to exterminate polygamy in Utah. Worst of all, it appears that this act of voting would seem to satisfy some consciences, even though this very vote should prolong the existence of that iniquitous institution. It would seem to satisfy some consciences — I will not call them stupid, or sluggish, or dead — that they voted against polygamy. Sir, if the ability of these gentlemen to execute were equal to their zeal to enact, we might almost say that omnipotence would be one of their weaknesses. But it is not proposed to execute; and there is no party in this country to-day, and there has been no party in this country during the last thirteen years, that would dare to vote bayonets and revolvers to shoot or stab polygamy out of Brigham Young and his followers. What, sir, do the Judiciary Committee ask us to do? What claim do they present for our votes in favor of this bill? What is claimed? Why, that the Congress of the United States should make an expression of opinion, so that the world may know that the United States of America are really opposed to polygamy? How much better, Mr. Speaker, we shall stand before the nations of the earth, when we shall have really shown them — what they may now be in doubt about — that we are actually opposed to polygamy? When we shall have shown it, not by doing any thing against the iniquity, but by a solemn vote, recorded upon the journals of this House!

Now, sir, I say that any such expression of sentiment is superfluous. There is no State in this Union that has not made polygamy a penal offence already; and what is the combined expression of the Representatives of these States, more than the individual expression of each of the States acting in its individual capacity? Do we by this combined action, add any thing to the force of all that separate action? Certainly not. The world understands now well enough that this country is opposed to polygamy, and it never will understand it any better by a vote of Congress, the whole effect of which will be to prolong the existence of that institution.

Then, sir, as an expression of sentiment, this bill is superfluous. But more than that. It is urged by some as a penal statute. Will it be enforced? I say no; and I tell you that, should the bill pass, neither you nor I will ever live to see a party which will dare to vote money and instruct the President to use it in putting in operation and in enforcing the penal statute which this bill proposes.

Then, sir, what does it amount to? I say, as a penal statute it is powerless. I will not go into the argument now to show why it ought not to be enforced, or the cruelty of attempting to enforce it against these men, who never could understand why the bill was enacted. I will not go into the argument about the expense of millions that it would cost this Government to enforce it; or that it would give the Mormons reason to charge that we have made use of persecution against them, driving them to the mountains and hunting them there like partridges, or that it would inevitably prolong the existence of the institution which it proposes to abolish. All these questions I pass by, for there is nobody here who claims that it is the purpose of any party to vote money or instructions to enforce this penal statute. .

But, sir, it is said that the honor and authority of the United States must be vindicated. The honor and authority of the United States vindicated, indeed, by a law which its very framers admit is, from its very inception, a dead letter! Nobody here now dare stand up and pledge his party to enforce this law. I challenge any man of any party to do that. I claim that it is a sham *ab initio ;* that it is a false pretence; and I never will vote for a sham or a false pretence, by whatever man or whatever party it may be brought into this House. I do not deal in such things, sir, especially upon practical questions like this now before us. The reasons that I have given are sufficient to govern my vote upon this bill, and that vote will be against it ; that, as an expression of the moral sense of the country, it is superfluous; that as a penal statute, it is powerless; that, as a vindication of the honor and authority of this Government, it is worse than futile ; for it would bring both the honor and authority of the Government into ridicule and contempt.

Now, sir, if these are facts, and if that is the prospect before us, should this bill be elevated to the dignity of a law by our votes?

Moral reformations should never be attempted by law, which can be accomplished without the aid of law. This would be true, even were the law proposed sure to effect the contemplated object, even if it were a law made and enforced by the political community where the offence existed. What excuse, then, can gentlemen give for a law like this, sure *not* to accomplish the object contemplated, made by a non-resident power, and intended never to be enforced?

Now, Mr. Speaker, let us inquire whether some act cannot be done which shall prove a perpetual and insurmountable barrier to the progress of this gigantic monstrosity. I am happy to be able to say that I believe that a solution — a peaceful, quiet, easy, natural, and practical solution — of this question is now within our reach. I am happy in the belief that the gold mines of Pike's Peak and the silver mines of Carson Valley do now furnish us a solution of this vexed question of polygamy. I have therefore proposed an amendment to this bill, that the Territory of Utah, together with a part of Kansas and Nebraska, shall be divided into two land districts, in such a way that the Mormon people shall be divided nearly equally between the two.

Now, sir, what are the facts about population? I come now to an argument which addresses itself directly to the judgment of the House, — an argument not of theories, but of facts. The Mormons, by the best intelligence, by the highest authority I can get, are to-day about forty thousand people. I have it from officers of the United States army who have been in Utah during the last two years, and they assure me that not more than one-seventh of this population of Mormons are voters. What are the facts in relation to the population of the two proposed land districts? I have the opinion of the Delegates from Jefferson, Kansas, and Nebraska, and numerous others, that there are now within the limits of the proposed land district of Jefferson forty thousand men, and that there are at least in that district twenty thousand voters; and we have it from papers last received from California, that there are now in Carson Valley at least thirty thousand men, and not less than fifteen thousand voters. I believe there has been a rapidity of increase of population in these districts which has no parallel in the history of this country; not even in the case of California. Why, sir, at the rate of increase now going on, it is confidently expected that at the next session of Congress these people will come here with the right to be admitted as sovereign States. Then, sir, you may defeat the policy of these Mormons at once, by erecting these land districts, which have already more than five times the voters of the Mormon population, and which population is rapidly increasing, while the number of Mormon voters is diminishing. With this prospect before us, is there any risk that Mormonism will not be exterminated by local law, provided we pass this amendment, constituting the land districts proposed? Would not a *local law* be much better to accomplish the purpose than a law made by a non-resident power? I contend that the law of a non-resident power is only fit to be laughed at and despised. The true authority, in my judgment, and the only authority worthy of being regarded, is the law that is made, approved, and enforced, by the people where it is law.

That local law is what Mormonism, polygamy, or any other crime, cannot evade. This non-resident law may do very well as capital for politicians; it may do for political pretences and shams; but it never will do for practice. I am not disposed to spend any time now in showing this House the inextricable difficulties and complications this precedent would lead us into if adopted. There is no end of them.

Do gentlemen propose that Congress shall follow up this mode of reforming all abuses that may occur upon the public lands of the United States? Shall we make laws against drunkenness, and profanity, and Sabbath-breaking, and larceny, — in short, shall we make a complete criminal code for our public lands, and establish a police and judicial force sufficient to arrest and convict and punish all offenders on this immense area? If this is to be our policy, then this bill proposes a good beginning. We shall probably have enough to do for some time to come, without attending at all to the legitimate purposes of the Government. Local law is the true remedy for these evils. The operation of such law, as contemplated in my amendment, will be sufficient for the speedy abolishment of polygamy.

Is it to be supposed that one hundred thousand miners at Pike's Peak, and the same number of miners at Carson Valley, without any women at all, will allow a monopoly of women at Salt Lake? [Laughter.] Sir, I do not agree with gentlemen who denounce these men in the Territories, these hardy pioneers, as men of no education, as men of no refinement, as men destitute of intelligence and moral power. I have never called them "runaways and outlaws." They are men of more vigor of body and of mind, of more heroism and enterprise, of more power of endurance, of more persistency, and of more character, than the people of the old States. They are also superior in intelligence to the average of the people in the old States. I doubt not, sir, that there are some educated men in Carson Valley, and some educated men in Pike's Peak; some who have read history, and some of them may have read Roman history. [Laughter.]

I feel perfectly secure, then, in the position that Mormonism and polygamy, and all things connected therewith, should be left to the local laws of the two land districts which I propose, by the action of Congress, to establish. Now, sir, is it safe to leave polygamy to the cure of a democracy? Is it safe to leave it to a republican form of government, made by the people themselves, in these two land districts? Every man acquainted with the history of the world knows that polygamy never has existed under a democratic or republican form of government. Every man who knows any thing, even without reading history, would decide beforehand that it never could exist under such a form of government while the sexes continue to be equal in numbers. Wherever it has existed, — in Turkey, in Arabia, among the chiefs of Central Africa, or among the aborigines of America, — it has always been protected by absolute military despotism. It can be sustained under no other system of government.

Then I hold that the argument is conclusive, that, by subjecting polygamy to the action of the democracy of these two land districts, it would most effectually put an end to it. This is one reason why I shall vote for the amendment to the bill as I have proposed it.

But it may be inquired, why we do not organize the Territories of Jefferson and Nevada, instead of simply constituting them land districts; why we do not pass an organic act. Now, sir, I am going to give my own views upon this subject; and I am going to say, for the amendment which I have proposed, that it neither affirms nor denies the power of Congress to legislate for the Territories. But while pursuing that course, I still hold my own views upon the subject; and if inquired of why I would not vote for a Territorial organization, my answer is ready; that I am opposed to the whole policy of organizing Territories by this Federal Government. I say here and now, that I will never vote,— as I believe I have never voted in the past,— to organize any Territory under this Government; neither would I acquire another foot of land to be governed by the Congress of the United States, or to be sold by the authority of this Government. The purposes of this Government are few and simple, as has been before said in this Hall. It is no part of the purpose for which this Government was organized, to exercise non-resident jurisdiction, or traffic in real estate; and therefore I am for getting rid of the nuisance, and of confining the Government to its legitimate purposes as soon as we can possibly do it. Therefore, again, I am opposed to the organization of any more Territories, and of inaugurating again the old policy of the Government, which has led to all the sectional quarrels which have existed, and now exist, between the States of the Union. I tell you we cannot afford to spend the time of this nation quarrelling about these provinces, which the Constitution does not know. The Constitution knows nothing less than a State; and why should we be forever quarrelling about Territories? Sir, I am so much a popular sovereignty man, that I deny that Congress can, by an organic act, bestow sovereignty upon the people of a Territory.

Mr. SMITH, of Virginia. Let me ask the gentleman a question. The gentleman says that the Constitution does not recognize anything else than a State. Then, what does he think of that clause of the Constitution which gives to Congress the power to dispose of the Territory and other property of the United States?

Mr. THAYER. I ought to have said, as a political community. The Constitution speaks of territory as property, as land; but, sir, as a political community it knows nothing less than a State. As a member of Congress, I would not be wiser than the Constitution. I am opposed even to granting permission to any Territory to make any laws, or to manage its own affairs in its own way. Why should

the citizens of Maine and Connecticut, of Georgia and South Carolina, and the other States, insult their equals in the Territories by the favor of granting them permission, through Congress, to govern themselves? Is a man who was a citizen of Iowa yesterday, and is to-day an inhabitant of Nebraska, less than the equal of him who remains a citizen and inhabitant of Iowa? How and why is his right of self-government impaired? No man can tell. If, then, he is the equal of any citizen of the States, it must be conceded that there is no occasion for the citizens of the States to graciously grant him equality of right.

No, sir; to grant permission to a Territory to make its own laws, implies authority which never rightfully existed in Congress. It implies the same authority as to command or to withhold permission. I will never vote such an insult to my fellow-citizens in a Territory. They are my equals in every right under this Government, and have just as good reason and authority to grant permission to their fellow-citizens in the States to govern themselves, as we in the States have to grant this permission by act of Congress to them.

Mr. SMITH, of Virginia. I want to ask another question. If Congress has no power over the Territory of the United States, except as property,—not as a political community,—then Congress has no power over the people of a Territory.

Mr. THAYER. Exactly, sir. It may be that, under the construction of the Constitution which has obtained, Congress would really be decided to have the same right to govern the people that George III. had to govern these colonies. I deny that it has now or ever had any moral right to govern American citizens in the Territories. To be explicit: if Congress has that right, where did it get it? Congress is the servant and not the king of the people. The people, Mr. Speaker, in this country, are king. There is no other. Nobody else has the attribute of sovereignty. If Congress can dispense sovereignty, certainly Congress has either acquired that sovereignty or has created it. Nobody believes that Congress creates sovereignty. If Congress acquired it, then when and where did it acquire it? Even the Church of Rome, absolute as is her authority, professes to give a reason for what she has and what she dispenses. When that church sells indulgences, she declares that she only sells the superabundant merit of the saints, so that men that are not as good as they ought to be, may have their deficiencies made up by men who are better than they need to be. [Laughter.] I would like to know where this superabundant sovereignty comes from, that Congress can dispense it. Only think what a reservoir of sovereignty this Congress must be, which has dispensed or pretends to have dispensed sovereignty to twenty sovereign States since the formation of this government, and has never had any sovereignty itself, except what it must have acquired from the sovereign people of this country. The fact is, Congress has never bestowed sovereignty upon one of them. It has only relinquished the sovereignty which it has usurped and withheld.

No, sir, this thing is a mistake. It is worse, — it is a fiction; it is a fallacy. The gentleman from Alabama [Mr. Curry], the other day, wondered by what *hocus-pocus*, by what legerdemain, that which is to-day public land becomes to-morrow a sovereignty. Public land does not become a sovereignty. Land never becomes a sovereignty. Men are the sovereigns.

If there is unoccupied public land to-day, and to-morrow there is a sovereignty upon it, I assure you that somebody has gone there — some citizen, who is himself so much above property that he alone is of more importance than all the public land that this Government ever did or ever will possess. He, sir, is the sovereign; and you disrobe him of his sovereignty because he has crossed a line and gone into a Territory. By what power, by what law, Congress being his servant — by what law can it be done? By just as good authority your coachman, sir, might put on your coat and hat, and command you to get upon the box and take the whip in hand, while he takes a seat inside the carriage.

But, sir, if the possession of land confers sovereignty, and if the sale of land implies the power to govern, I would like to know whether the selling of the products of the land does not give the right to govern the buyers? I would like to know whether the doctrine that the party, whether the government or an individual, who sells land, thereby acquires the right to govern the purchasers of the land, is any more ridiculous than the assumption that the grain dealer who sells corn, the product of the land, thereby acquires the right to govern his customers?

Such a grain dealer as this was Pharaoh, who bought his people with corn. When the years of famine had rendered the land unproductive, and therefore worthless, the basis of absolute sovereignty was changed from land to the products of the land. Sovereignty just as much attaches, and with just as good right, to the one as to the other. The assumption that it belongs to either, or to the owner of either, on account of possession, or of sale, is simple ridiculous.

Land is nothing but property. The fiction, that the possession of land gives sovereignty, and the right to govern people who are upon it, is a part of the old feudal system. We have everywhere connected with the fibers of this government some of the relics of ancient tyranny. When William the Conqueror invaded and subdued England, he proclaimed that the fee of all the land on the island was in himself, and he parcelled it out among his retainers. Holding possession of the land, he then proclaimed that all the men who lived upon it were his slaves. And from the old feudal system we derive this ancient, this fallacious idea, that the possession of land by this government gives it the power to govern anybody who shall buy the land. I have no sympathy with any such thing. I detest it now, and I shall detest it always, and use my influence against it.

Mr. Speaker, while I advocate these views, the amendment I propose commits no man who may vote for it to them; for that amendment neither affirms nor denies the power of Congress to legislate hereafter for these land districts which are thereby constituted. I hope I have succeeded in showing that the bill which is proposed will not accomplish the purpose which it professes to have in view. I hope I have succeeded in showing that we are able, by a natural and effective method, to accomplish these results. I might have spoken of the complications which this territorial policy is ever imposing upon the government, and of the dangerous consolidation of power to which these complications inevitably lead. A Republic never can successfully govern provinces. Whenever it has attempted to do it, the history of the world has shown that it has not only failed, but it has been overthrown by that policy. The policy of acquiring and of governing provinces creates a necessity for an army and a navy. It is to make the President of the United States, to all intents and purposes, a king; and I am, therefore, for abolishing this policy as soon as may be.

You remember, sir, that it was upon this very mission of acquiring and governing provinces, that Julius Cæsar had been in Gaul, when returning, he crossed the Rubicon with his army, and overthrew the liberties of his country.

Similar to that has been the history of every Republic which has attempted to exercise non-resident jurisdiction—that has attempted to acquire and govern provincial dependencies. While I am willing to annex sovereignties at the right time, I protest against the acquisition of territory, to be governed or sold by Congress. I am for simplifying the operations of the government in respect to the Territories. We have the land to sell. Let us provide for selling it; but beyond that I would not recommend action. Let the people take care of themselves. They are the sovereigns. Congress is their servant.

A bill had been introduced into the House for the organization of new Territories, upon which speeches were made, with others, by Mr. Gooch of Mass., and Mr. Curtis of Iowa. These gentlemen were advocates of the old method of organization, with its executive appointments, its Indian wars, and its endless disputes in Congress over the control of the inhabitants. It afforded Mr. Thayer, therefore, an excellent opportunity to present his statement of the only practical way in which Territorial affairs are hereafter to be disposed of, which he improved to the utmost, in a speech delivered on the 11th of May. He takes broad ground, in this speech, for *the people themselves*, and for the supremacy of *free labor:* believing that population and not politicians, will hereafter settle all disputes of a local character, which have become, by Congressional interference, the greatest national nuisances that afflict us. This speech abounds with irony, humor, and wit, and its main positions are very strongly taken. It is as follows:—

Mr. Speaker: I have listened with great interest to the remarks of my colleague, and also to those of the gentleman from Iowa [Mr. Curtis]. They have manifested suitable ingenuity in the discussion of this question; for, sir, it is the work of giants to prove to the people of this country that they have not a right to govern themselves, and that Congress has a right to govern them. That is a work that can be done only by giants. It is easy for ordinary men, for common men, to show to the people of this country that they have the right to govern themselves, and that they are abundantly prepared to exercise that right. In the early history of this Government, we had the Providence Plantations, the Plymouth colony, and the Connecticut colony, which drummed out a Governor forced upon them by a non-resident power, and thereby secured to that State an indestructible possession—the proud history of the charter oak. Those men from the old country formed upon our soil model governments, and they did it without ever having had the experience afforded by the exercise of self-government.

But, sir, it is contended that we, who have always governed ourselves, when we go to a Territory of the United States are unable to tell our hands from our feet. It is contended that a man not only loses his rights, but loses his common sense, by going to a Territory. The gentleman from Iowa ——

Mr. Curtis. Mr. Speaker ——

Mr. Thayer. I will allow no interruption. The gentleman from Iowa refused to let me ask him a question. I remember that.

Mr. Curtis. I certainly did not, or, at least, I did not intend it.

Mr. Thayer. I shall not be interrupted. I have the floor.

Mr. Curtis. I did not hear the gentleman, if he asked me any question.

Mr. Thayer. I was not astonished at the surprise which my colleague manifested, that I had taken the lead in this business of killing off these Territorial organizations, which go upon the assumption that the people of a Territory are infants. Therefore, I could understand the grief which he and the gentleman from Iowa must have felt when they saw that this leading and this voting was successful in the accomplishment of that result. Rachel mourned for her first-born, and would not be comforted. This day's slaughter of the innocents is, no doubt, an appropriate cause and occasion of grief.

Sir, grief may have a salutary influence upon men. The efforts of ingenuity and of invention may quicken their intellects. I am glad to see gentlemen striving for arguments that do not exist, and can never be found, showing why Congress shall make an organic law for the people of the Territories, who are a thousand times better able than Congress to understand their wishes and necessities. There was need, sir, in this work, of quick and ready invention, of nervous struggling for expedients. We have witnessed all that this day—

"All the soul in rapt suspension;
All the quivering, palpitating
Chords of life in utmost tension
With the fervor of invention,
With the rapture of creating."

I said, grief itself may be salutary; and when these gentlemen see that they are in the minority, and that we who oppose their favorite measures are a majority in this House, I sympathize with them. I know something about the effect of defeat; and I say it, for their consolation, that I think it may be good. Sir, I have known something of the feeling of men who have experienced defeat; this feeling of distrust of the power of Providence to carry forward a good cause, this loss of faith in men, this ruinous and apparently crushing despair, may, sometimes, work great good. The pearl is only the crystallized tear of the oyster.

Mr. Gooch rose.

Mr. Thayer. I will not be interrupted.

Mr. Gooch. I say to my colleague, that I allowed him to interrupt me frequently during my remarks on the polygamy bill, a few days ago; and yet he is not willing to give me the same privilege.

Mr. Thayer. If my colleague wishes to interrupt me, I will allow him to do any thing he chooses. [Laughter.]

Mr. Gooch. I thought that my colleague would not be as unjust as he intimated. I must express some surprise at the reference my colleague has made. If he had looked up his quotations to express surprise, instead of grief, it would have been more to the purpose. I expressed no grief. I simply expressed surprise.

Mr. Thayer. I have not looked up any quotations. I happen generally to know what is appropriate, without looking them up. [Laughter.]

Now, Mr. Speaker, let me say further to my colleague, whose grief and surprise I trust may be for his spiritual and eternal good, that I will give him another quotation to the same point:

"Such a fate as this was Dante's—
By *defeat* and exile maddened;
Thus were Milton and Cervantes,
Nature's priests, and Corybantes,
By *affliction touched and saddened*."

And again:

"Only those are crowned and sainted,
Who with grief have been acquainted."

Now, sir, let us look for a moment at the arguments which have been sought after to show that Congress should organize Territorial governments. I will now leave the region of the sensibilities, and visit, for a time, the domain of the intellect—a movement from what is sublime in feeling in my opponents, to what is ridiculous in reason. I understand, Mr. Speaker, that those arguments have all been made on a proposition to organize a Territory which has no white men in it. There is not a member of the Committee on Territories who has spoken, or who will rise and say that there are three hundred white men in the Territory of Chippewa.

Mr. Grow. Oh, yes, there are.

Mr. Aldrich. If the gentleman will go there, he will find a good many more than three hundred white men there. The gentleman lives so far off, it is not to be wondered at that he should make such a statement.

Mr. Thayer. I had it from the contesting Delegate from Nebraska.

Mr. Clark of Missouri. I desire to ask the chairman of the Committee on Territories if there has been any petition signed by any man within the limits of Chippewa Territory, in favor of an organization of that Territory; and what evidence they have that there are even one hundred and eighty white men within its limits?

Mr. Smith of Virginia. I do not believe there is one white man there.

Mr. Grow. I should like to ask the gentleman from Missouri what petitions there were from Kansas and Nebraska at the time those Territories were organized?

Mr. Houston. Oh, that is no argument! One wrong does not justify another.

Mr. Thayer. Now, let me make one remark to the gentleman from Iowa, who appealed to this House, to afford protection to these infants in the Territories ——

Mr. Curtis. I hope the gentleman will allow me to correct his statement.

Mr. Thayer. The gentleman did not allow me.

Mr. Curtis. I certainly did not refuse to allow the gentleman to interrupt me, to correct any thing I might have said. If the gentleman appealed to me, and I did not yield to him, it was because I did not hear him, and not from any want of courtesy. Now, sir, I protest that I never spoke of the people of the Territories as infants. I spoke of them as men; and if I used the word "infant" in that connection, it was to characterize the Territories as infant empires.

Mr. Thayer. I was not talking of the gentleman's orthography or etymology. I was talking about his speech.

Mr. Curtis. I used no expression of the kind.

Mr. Thayer. I was not quoting the gentleman in words; I was talking about his argument, which was to show that the people of the Territories were wholly unable to take care of themselves, and that they must be afforded protection by the General Government. What do they want with our protection? And if they do want it, what protection would they get except a government of broken-down politicians, which the President of the United States would send them? They have King Log now; they would have King Stork then. Is a Governor a ten-horse power to protect the people? So far from that, sir, he is as much inferior to the hardy pioneer, in strength and character, as Lombardy poplar is to live oak. What is there in such a Governor? What is there in such a secretary? What is there in such marshals? What is there in a whole force of Territorial officers such as would be sent there to protect the people? Depend upon it, if they are protected at all, they will protect themselves; nobody else will protect them; and besides that, they must protect all these government officials, if we send them. I ask, who are the men you would send there? Men whom the people have defeated at home. These are the men usually sent to govern the Territories; these are the governmental officials, under whatever party jurisdiction appointed; and they have usually been worse to the people of the Territories than the frogs and lice to the people of Egypt. [Laughter.]

But, sir, to carry the illustration further: Here the people are the sovereigns; these nuisances go up into the chambers of the kings. Why do they go? To fill their own pockets with the gold of the General Government; to trade with the Indians; to speculate in town lots; and often, one of the methods by which they accomplish their ends is by stirring up Indian wars. I have appealed to our history to show that the people can govern themselves, and I might as well go on a little further in the same direction. It does happen that the people of the State of Oregon were, during the first ten years of their history, without a Territorial Government. Their first Governor, Gen. Lane, has said that the people of Oregon had not since been under so good laws, so well enforced, as they made for themselves, before the time when their Government received the sanction of Congress. They had done every thing that pertained to good government. Still, there are men who will stand up here and say, that without a Territorial organization by Congress, the people would be ruined.

Now, sir, I tell you what is the object of these Territorial organizations. It is to make the people believe that nothing on this continent can be done without Congress. It is an attempt to deify the politician at the expense of the people; that is the whole of it. Sir, do you think that this House of Representatives, that this Senate, that this President, is the motive power of this government? If you do, let me assure you, you know but little about it. The motive power of this government is the people—the people at home, who attend to their own business and mind their own matters — and the politicians here, who pretend that they themselves are the motive power, are insignificant in comparison with the fly on the axletree, who claimed that he made the coach move. [Laughter.] That is the fact. Now, sir, I am tired of these assumptions. I cannot endure them. I contend that it is better to leave these men alone, without our supervision, until their faults or weaknesses shall show that our intervention alone can be their salvation.

I think, now, Mr. Speaker, that I have vindicated the power of the people to govern themselves. I have shown it as it appears in our history. These people of Dakota are as well off to-day as they would be if they had our Territorial officials over them. They have now no Indian wars. The Yanctons and the Sioux are all quiet. But organize the Territory, and send out your executive officials; and then, sir, these speculators will greatly desire an influx of government gold. There is no method so sure and so convenient to produce that result, as to stir up an Indian war. It will be done, sir, to raise the price of town lots. The Yanctons and Sioux will come down on the white settlements, and we shall soon hear of the terrible inroads of the savages. Then, sir, a heart-rending appeal for protection. Then, sir, a regiment of soldiers and $1,000,000. Then, sir, damages and pensions and war claims to the end of time. They are better off to-day, than they can be with these government speculators turned loose upon them.

Mr. GOOCH. I wish to ask my colleague whether he recognizes the right of Congress to interfere, if the people of a Territory should frame institutions which, in its opinion, were improper, and not in accordance with the theory and spirit of this government?

Mr. THAYER. Our fathers had a general rule, which they applied very frequently when questions were asked about what they would do in certain contingencies; and that rule was, that they would answer any such questions when they should arise in practice. That is a very good rule for me to act upon in this case.

Mr. GOOCH. Does not my colleague consider that such a question may have arisen in the case of Utah, and perhaps in the case of New Mexico?

Mr. THAYER. No case has yet arisen in practice. No evil has yet been consummated in the Territories, which the people there, by their own local laws, are not abundantly able to remove.

Now, sir, I do not propose to have any thing to say concerning the negro in the bills which I shall offer to the House. I am perfectly willing that, for a time under this government, the negro as well as the sovereignty of Congress, shall be held in abeyance. Perhaps that is the reason why some gentlemen are surprised, and why they grieve. It may be that, if my colleague were not surprised at me, I should be very much surprised at

myself. You will remember, in the beginning of this session of Congress, that assurances were given by many Republicans here, that this question of slavery should not be introduced by them during the present Congress. I, sir, was one of the Republicans who repeatedly gave that assurance to men whose votes were doubtful; and had it not been for such assurance, you, to-day, Mr. Speaker, would not be occupying the position of presiding officer of this House. Sir, such an assurance was publicly given upon this floor by the Republican candidate for Speaker [Mr. Sherman], and that assurance was quoted by the gentleman from Maryland [Mr. Davis], in his defence against the resolutions of the Maryland Legislature, that the Republicans would not introduce the question of slavery into this House. I have honestly observed my promise in reference to the assurance which I gave men whose votes were doubtful on the question of the Speakership.

Mr. Speaker, I do not propose, in the organization of these Territories, to agitate the country with that question. There is no manner of need of it. I have said before that the interests of freedom do not demand it. I say now, that the interests of slavery do not demand it. What do the fanatics in both sections of this country want? They know that the whole country is tired of the question. If the whole country could respond to-day as one man, they would say so. Have we nothing else to look after in this country but the slavery question? Is there nothing here but "Northern aggression" and "Southern aggression?" Are all the glorious achievements in our history forgotten? Are all the momentous interests of our present condition of no importance? But, sir, these fanatics, both in the North and in the South, know nothing, see nothing, care for nothing, but the negro question.

Above us is the broad expanse of heaven, filled with glowing constellations;

"In reason's ear they all rejoice,
And utter forth a glorious voice."

There is "Arcturus with his sons," and Orion with the Pleiades; but we have a set of one-idea men in the North, who can see nothing in the whole canopy, save the "Twins," and another set of cognate fanatics in the South, who can see nothing but the "Bear circling the Pole." Poor men! They sit up nights — the one class'to see that the " Bear " does not devour the " Twins," and the other class to see that the " Twins " do not set some trap for the "Bear!" A fine help are these haggard night-watchers to the great Eternal ! Their " eternal vigilance," no doubt, prevents a collision of the planets. How thankful we should be that such self-sacrificing heroes still live ! We all know well enough what might happen, if even one little world should be jostled out of place.

" Let but *one* planet from its orb be hurled,
Planets and suns rush lawless through the world."

There was one man, Newton, who comprehended all these constellations and the laws which govern them. He weighed worlds. He gave to mortals the grandest law of the physical universe. He could see the whole ethereal expanse, and contemplate it, and scrutinize its movements, and almost fathom its mysteries. But Pope says of that Titanic intellectual prodigy :

" Superior beings, when of late they saw
A mortal man unfold all nature's law,
Admired such wisdom in the human shape,
And showed a Newton as we show an ape."

If, sir, "superior beings" saw a Newton as an ape, by what multiplication of microscopic power could they see at all a little dwarfed politician, who himself can see but one constellation, or at most two, in the whole handiwork of Jehovah, and these two the " Bear " and the " Twins ? " [Great laughter.]

Let me say to the gentlemen from the South who are sensitive on this question of slavery, that a sublimer faith would become great men. Those men especially who say that slavery is of Divine origin. Why, Mr. Speaker, who is the author of Divine institutions ? " It is He who sitteth upon the circuit of the heavens, and before Him all the inhabitants of the earth are as grasshoppers." If, then, he has established certain relations between grasshoppers of one color and grasshoppers of another color, be assured those relations will stand any and all tests. Who can overthrow them ? Can the North ? [Great laughter.] Is my colleague going to do it ? I think not; for these things which have the superintendence and approval of Almighty God are above even these giants who contend against the right of the people

to govern themselves. The Titans even could not dethrone Jupiter.

The appeal is made to us from every reason of philanthrophy, from every sentiment of pity, that those " poor people " in the Territories may not be allowed to govern themselves, for the reason that they cannot pay their own expenses. Well, sir, if they cannot do it, is it not as easy for us to appropriate money to govern the land districts, or to aid them in governing themselves, as it is to appropriate money to pay the officials which the Executive may send out ? What man can doubt that ? If they are in such a strait as to want assistance in their government, who is here so base as to refuse to give it. There is no party here, there has been no party in this country, but what would listen to the appeals of these people, coming with this plea of poverty that they were unable to meet the legitimate expenses of their government; they would have an appropriation ; and one-half of the ordinary appropriation would be better for them, paid to their own citizens; whom they would elect to these offices, than the whole appropriation paid to Federal officials, who go out to the Territories only for a temporary residence, and who return with the profits of their proconsulship to settle in Fifth avenue, or in some of the Eastern cities. Under this mode of allowing the people to govern themselves, they will select their own fellow-citizens, residents in the same Territory ; and these officers will receive their salaries, not to be transported to Eastern cities to be spent in luxury; but, sir, to be used in building up the young Territories, and the future States which shall be made within her limits.

Mr. Speaker, another objection of my colleague is, that there can be no law except mob law among these people in the Territories. I have shown that in our earliest colonies, without the advantage of former experience in self-government, the people have made models of government for themselves. I have shown that the people of Oregon have made model institutions without the advice or sanction of Congress. My colleague says that nothing but mob law can exist, except where this omniscient Legislature shall show the world some nobler achievements. Mob law, made by infants, and I suppose carried out by infants! No, sir; mob law made by sensible men, your equals and mine, from your State and from mine; every one of them abundantly able to draw up a bill of rights or a Constitution. And these are the men who know nothing but mob law, and this Congress should exercise its all-wise influence to restrain them from self-destruction, from annihilation ! Is it possible, sir, that, in this age of the world, there is any man so big a fool as to suppose that Anglo-Saxons have not in themselves the elements of self-preservation? If there is, sir, he ought to be schooled a while longer by his mother and by his nurse. I contend, sir, that Anglo-Saxons, wherever you find them, have the elements of self-government and the elements of self-preservation. Put them down where you please, in small numbers or in great numbers, familiar friends or strangers to each other, and they will institute a perfect code of laws, and they will enforce them. Personal rights, rights of property, all rights, will be protected under those laws.

Now, sir, this is a scheme to deify politicians, and that is why it is fought for. What will the politicians do, these men ask, when it is seen all over the country that the people can do without them, and without their supervision and parental care in Congress? " Othello's occupation " will be gone, and especially the occupation of such Othellos as have their all invested in Wilmot Provisos or Congressional intervention in some shape. What can they do when the people shall have said, as they will say, that no provisos are necessary, and no Congressional intervention consistent with the principles and policy of this Government. I take the stand that any such proviso or any such intervention is in direct antagonism to the Declaration of Independence, which says that " all Governments derive their just powers from the consent of the governed." Is that the kind of government which this Congress of the United States, without one word of authority from the people, imposes, — to tell them how they shall act and what they shall do in the Territories? Do you claim, Mr. Speaker, that you have a right to say that a man in Washington Territory, whose wife is dead, shall not have the right to marry his former wife's sister? Do you pretend to say at what time they shall dig clams in Washington Territory? [Laughter.] Who pretends to say that it is the business of Congress to go into all these minutiæ; to direct every movement, control every wish,

shape every expression of the will of the people of the Territories of the United States? Whoever pretends to say so, is not entitled to have much influence among American citizens.

Mr. Gooch. I wish merely to say to my colleague, that it seems to me he is fighting a proposition which nobody ever did assume. Nobody has assumed such a proposition here to-day, as that Congress could do any thing of that kind ; but merely that we should give a helping hand to the people, in organizing their local government, which may do these things.

Mr. Thayer. I perfectly well understand all that. It is to give a helping hand to the politicians, not to the people; that is what my colleague wants. He is afraid I will lose my place in this House for not lending a helping hand. I do not fear any such thing, so long as I adhere to what I can defend by good logic. I do not fear to go before the people of any part of the country with this as my thesis: that the people are supreme in this Government, and that they have the right to govern themselves.

Mr. Gooch. I desire to ask my colleague whether he means to say that I have ever intimated any such thing as he suggests?

Mr. Thayer. What?

Mr. Gooch. That I was afraid you would lose your place here on account of your position on this or any other question.

Mr. Thayer. I suppose that, on account of your abundant sympathy, that was the case.

Mr. Gooch. When the gentleman cannot find something that exists to fight, he fights something that does not exist.

Mr. Thayer. If the gentleman wishes me to come directly to the point, I will do so. He says Congress has the power to govern the people ; and he complains because I said that Congress might exercise that power by telling the people of a country when they were to dig clams, and when not ; and might exercise it by saying whether a man might marry his former wife's sister or not. Now, I ask my colleague if he denies that Congress has the power to say both these things?

Mr. Gooch. What I say in regard to the matter is this: that it is the duty of Congress merely to assist these people in organizing a Territorial government; not to dictate to them their measures of legislation, only so far as that they shall not legislate in such a way as would be against the best interests of the people of the Territory and the whole country.

What I mean to say, still further, is, that if a Territorial Legislature shall pass any law which in the judgment of Congress shall be contrary to the policy or theory of our government, or which in the end would place this Territory in such a condition that it would not be a proper subject to be received into the Union on an equality with the other States, then it is the duty of Congress to interfere and prohibit or repeal such law ——

Mr. THAYER. I think my colleague has gone on far enough.

Mr. GOOCH. Then I will sit down.

Mr. THAYER. That is right. I would like to know what kind of philosophy it is that my colleague's views are based upon. Is it the philosophy of persecution and proscription, or is it the philosophy of Christianity? Does he suppose, when the people of a Territory are determined to act in a certain way, and to exercise certain rights, that by legislating here to the contrary he can prevent their acting in that certain way, and exercising those certain rights? Is he of the opinion that he is going to convert these men to what he considers right, by force? Is that his idea? Does he expect that if they love slavery and hate freedom, he is going to make them good Christians and good freedom-men by legislating that they never shall have slaves? Would he propose, in respect to Christianizing Hindostan that the best method for the missionary societies would be to send over and steal their idols? Would he make them Christians any sooner by legislating in Massachusetts, or here in the Federal government, against idol worship in Hindostan? No, sir, that is entirely a wrong philosophy. You cannot legislate religion, or temperance, or Christianity, or heaven, into any people under the sun. No, sir; this must be accomplished by other means. Converts are not made, especially in this country, by force. But, sir, it seems to be the cherished opinion of some, that there is no other way of making converts to any thing good, except legislation. Now, I have a philosophy about government, and the duties of government, which cannot by any possibility accord with the views expressed by my colleague. The proposition that I make, as com-

prehending that whole philosophy, are very simple and are only two in number. These are, first, that the first duty of the government is to let the people alone; and, second, that its second duty is to prevent my colleague, or anybody else from interfering with them. [Laughter.]

Now, sir, if they are unable to work out their own salvation, it is putting very great burdens, Mr. Speaker, on you and me, to work out the salvation of all the people of this country. You and I might be the only men who understand in what line and in what direction this great salvation lies. How shall we accomplish it with the perverse wills of the whole nation against us?

Now, I will state to you what is the radical and distinctive difference between parties in this country; and there can be traced to this radical distinction every measure which occasions any conflict in this House or in the country. That radical distinction is this: faith in the people, and no faith in the people. It so happens, and it wisely happens, that no party will ever control, or has ever controlled, this government, but what either exercises this faith in the people, or makes the people believe that it exercises it. [Laughter.]

Now, sir, I challenge any man to controvert that maxim. It has not been done here, and it cannot be done here. I will meet, now, or at any time, any man on these radical propositions of government which I now enunciate. If my colleague wishes now to make any explanation of his views, I will listen to him. [Laughter.]

Mr. GOOCH. I have as much belief in the ability of the people to govern themselves as my colleague or any other man has; but, sir, when I look to our Territories, I say that those Territories belong to the people of the whole country; that in those Territories every individual in the country has an interest; and I believe that no ten men, or twenty men, or one hundred men, from the United States, or from any foreign country, have a right to go there and build up precisely such institutions as they please; to organize, if they choose, a monarchical form of government, and build up institutions which shall make the States to be formed out of those Territories unfit ever to be taken into the Union.

Mr. THAYER. Now I understand all that my colleague is going to say. [Laughter.] Mr. GOOCH. Then my colleague does not want my views. He has had enough of them. Mr. THAYER. I understand all that he is going to say. His propositions are these: first, that every man in this country has an equal right to the territory of the United States, and therefore his inference is this: that every man in this country has a right to impress his own peculiar views upon the people who shall occupy that Territory. Mr. GOOCH. No; my colleague mistakes my theory. My theory is, that the people, as a whole, own the Territories; that the views of the different individuals shall be placed together; and, that the sum of all the opinions of all the people shall prevail in the Territories.

Mr. THAYER. Well, now, that would work very great hardship in case there should be nine hundred and ninety-nine men of one view, and one thousand men of the other. The nine hundred and ninety-nine, who, according to his assertion, have an equal right in the Territories, would, by the action of one man, have no rights whatever.

Mr. GOOCH. The theory of our government is, that the majority shall govern. Does my colleague deny that?

Mr. THAYER. And all this, Mr. Speaker, after the people in the Territories have bought their land and paid for it! After that, these men have a right to impress them with their peculiar views on politics, religion, on moral and mental philosophy, on spiritualism, and what not. There is no end to what we might make topics of legislation. Well, I am not for making these things topics of legislation myself; and if I had my way about it, a poet never would write a platform for the Republican party. [Laughter.] I do not like metaphors in platforms. I want them prose: or, if they must be poetry, I would like to have them very good poetry.

Now, from what source can this power be derived, that enables men who have sold these lands to people who are their equals in every respect—who are citizens of the United States—where is the power derived from, that gives to men in Maine, and Massachusetts, and Iowa, the right to say what institutions the pioneers shall have? But I am told, with grave solemnity, by my colleague, that this is the ancient policy of this govern-

ment. It is not so ancient as Satan. [Laughter.] It is not so old as Sin, the daughter of Satan. Its age is no reason why it should be forever sustained. It is old enough to die.

Mr. GOOCH. I desire to ask my colleague whether he intends to place the framers of our government, and the men who engrafted this policy on the Territories, in the same category with the distinguished individual to whom he has referred, and to say that their work is on a par with what he terms sin? [Laughter.]

Mr. THAYER. No, sir, neither them nor my colleague. I have no idea of doing such a thing. But I do say of the men who framed this government, that they might not have been perfect, even in human wisdom; and I do say, contrary perhaps to the opinion of many, that the present generation is not less wise than the past. It may sound strangely, but any man who denies it denies faith in God and human nature. No, sir; I contend that we are degenerate men, unless we can inaugurate a better policy than that which has been inaugurated one or two centuries ago. Have we not improved on the law of promogeniture? Have we not improved upon the feudal system? But this idea, that Congress have the right to govern the Territories because they have sold the lands to the people who live there is a part of that system.

No, sir; I tell you that this Territorial policy has been, from the outset, progressing all the while in favor of popular rights. The first stage in our Territorial policy was, that the President should send out the executive power, the legislative power, and the judicial power, for every Territory. That was the first policy. The second policy was, that the President should send out the executive power, the judicial power, and a part of the legislative power—the Council—while the people of the Territory might elect the lower branch of the Legislature. The third step of our Territorial policy was this: that the President should send out the executive and judicial powers, while the people of the Territory should elect the whole legislative power. And, sir, the fourth step in our policy was—and that was the Kansas-Nebraska bill—that Congress should not have intervention for the revision of the laws which the people in a Territory should make, although by that act the sovereignty of the people in the Territory was held in abeyance during their Territorial condition, subject to the sovereignty of the President.

Now, sir, the step which I propose, which is the fifth step in our Territorial policy, is this: that the sovereignty of the people shall be active, and not held in abeyance, while the sovereignty of the President and the sovereignty of Congress shall be held in abeyance. This, sir, is the fifth and last step in our Territorial policy.

" Time's noblest offspring is her last."

This policy, sir, is the *Ultima Thule* of popular sovereignty—the pillars of Hercules, sir, on which I now write, in letters so that the world may read, " THE NE PLUS ULTRA OF ANGLO-SAXON GOVERNMENT."

But, sir, I will not censure my colleague for entertaining any fears for the safety of free institutions, which he may choose to cherish. I can understand how he and other men—not, perhaps, of the most bold and defiant disposition — may claim that there is danger of slavery's grasping and destroying all our Northern rights. I have heard of an old man who had read what Herschel had said about the spots on the sun — that they were increasing; and, sir, he looked at the sun, to see whether the spots continued to increase; and he kept looking, till he could see nothing but one black spot; and then he died of grief, thinking the sun had gone out, when he had only gone out himself. [Great laughter.] These timid men in the Northern States, who believe that slavery is going to overspread the continent, and swallow up Canada and Massachusetts, get blinded by the dazzling light of all our free institutions and the glory of our nation's progress and history, and they can see nothing but a black spot that covers the whole, and, therefore, they fill the whole earth with their mourning. [Laughter.] Now, I am not of that class of men. I tell you, sir, that, reading the history of this country, I can in no way convince myself that, by all these providential triumphs over British aggressions, by all these providences in our behalf during our whole history, God has preserved and cherished this nation, just for the purpose of allowing it to be submerged and destroyed by disunion, or slavery, or by any other calamity whatever.

Now, sir, I have faith in the people of every section of the country. I do not be-lieve that the problem which belongs exclusively to the people of Texas, or exclusively to the people of Louisiana, can, by any possibility, be worked out to a satisfactory and correct result by the people of Massachusetts or the people of Maine. And as to the question of slavery in these States, I believe that the Northern people have no more business with it than we have with the laws of primogeniture in England, or than we have with the institutions of China, Hungary, or Turkey. Not one whit more. We are a Congress of nations, to all intents and purposes; we have no business each with the sovereignty of another, nor the sovereignty of the whole with the individual rights of any one. There can, then, be no quarrel between the North and the South concerning slavery in the States. We can only have that apple of discord in our Territorial governments. I have, therefore, said not one word about it in the land district system which I have presented to the House and to the country. I have observed my promise, in them, not to bring the agitation of the slavery question into the House. That was my promise, and I will observe it.

But my colleague says we must send out suitable men to govern these Territories. I suppose they have no suitable men there ! I suppose no man in one of these unorganized Territories ever heard of such a place as the State of Massachusetts, or that my colleague was a Representative of that State ! and what do they know, if they do not know *that?* [Laughter.] Suitable men ! Men who cannot get a living at home ; men who have not popularity enough to be re-elected in their own districts. Suitable men ! Who are the men who are there ? They are men who have travelled across the mountains ; who have hunted wild beasts; who have fought the Indians; who understand human nature better than any man can possibly do who is a member of this House, from the experience of a quiet life. These are the men whom some little puckered-up lawyer in Maine or Massachusetts, with his feet upon the window-sill, calls "infants," while he prates about "*our* parental care." [Great laughter.]

Now, sir, I have no kind of patience with this kind of argument, which goes before the country assailing the character of the men of the Territories. But if this were all, I might submit to it; but, adding insult to injury, it assails their common sense; it assails their manhood, calls them "interlopers, runaways, and outlaws," and in every way wholly unfit for civilization and self-government. What on earth did God make such men for? Now, sir, I will yield to my colleague, if he wishes. [Laughter.]

Mr. Gooch. My colleague has been indulging in his usual style of fighting wind-mills.

Mr. Thayer. I was fighting my *colleague*, Mr. Speaker.

Mr. Gooch. My colleague has not stated any argument or remark of mine. What I said was, not that these men were inferiors; I said they were men just as capable of governing themselves as the people of any other portion of the country. But I said that, at the outset of a Territorial organization, they had little or no knowledge of each other; that they were too few and scattered to enable them to select proper officers from among themselves; and that, for the purpose of starting a government, they should have the aid of the General government, and that their first executives should be selected by the General government, instead of being selected by those men, whom I admitted might be the equals of my colleague and myself. I wish my colleague would reply to what I did say, instead of replying to his own fancies, to his own windmills, which he sets up for himself.

Mr. Thayer. The House shall judge whether I am dealing fairly with my colleague. There shall be no mistake this time. I understand him this time to make two statements: one is, that the people are too few and scattered in the Territories for them to establish a government for themselves. Is that correct? [Mr. Gooch nodded assent.] The other is, that they are strangers. Is that right? [Mr. Gooch again nodded assent.]

Now, sir, with the leave of the House, I shall answer both these propositions. The first, that the people are too few in numbers: let me ask my colleague if there is more danger of the overthrow of good government in the town of Paxton, which is one of the smallest in my county, or in the town of Hull, one of the towns near Cape Cod, which, I believe, has about seventy-five people, than there is in the city of New York, or in the city of Baltimore? Did my colleague ever hear of a riot or a rebellion in the patriotic town of Hull? Has he not often heard of riots in New York and Baltimore? I put it to this House, whether the fewness in number of the people of a Territory is a strong reason why the government of the United States should interfere and see that they should not blot themselves out? Why, every man knows that our republican institutions are in the most danger where the population is the most dense. Has my colleague any thing to say to that?

Mr. Gooch. My idea is, that there is more danger of institutions formed in the organization of a government where there are few men who participate in that organization, than where it is participated in by many. And again, every one knows that the people who go to an unorganized Territory go from different countries, and many of them come from foreign countries; and I say that there is more danger that institutions will be established there not in accordance with the theory of our government, than where there is a larger collection of people.

Mr. Thayer. I feel the whole force of that argument. My colleague has shown that if there was only one man in a Territory, there would be very great danger of a mob there, and an overthrow of republican institutions. [Laughter.] Has the gentleman ever read the history of France? Has he ever heard of barricades in the streets of Paris? Has he ever read Roman history; and does he not know that all dangers to government occur where the people are the most dense, where they are packed, where they exist in crowds? My colleague certainly knows all that; I will not take the position of denying that he knows all that. How, then, can he, with a knowledge of the history of this country and of all countries, claim that there is the greatest danger to republican institutions or to good government where there are the fewest people? The fact, — and every man knows it, — is, that where there are few people, there never was, and there never can be, any great danger.

My colleague's other proposition is, that the people are strangers to each other. Does my colleague suppose these Yankees are like the Frenchman, who would not save a drowning man because he had not been introduced to him? [Laughter.] Does my colleague suppose the Yankees have not the power of getting acquainted ? If they had no social qualities whatever, they would see if something could not be made out of an acquaintance. [Great laughter.] Does my colleague deny that ? [Continued laughter.]

Mr. Gooch. I do not deny that, if they will only let my colleague get up an organized scheme of emigration, and put the Yankees there, for he would select the right kind.

Mr. Thayer. I will do my whole duty in that regard. [Laughter.] Now, Mr. Speaker, what is there in this humbug of Congressional intervention that commends itself to the people of this country ? Nothing. Neither you, sir, nor myself, will live to see another Territory organized by this government to govern our fellow-citizens, equal to you and to me, in the Territories of this Union. The vote in this House to-day has shown that the people are tired of intervention, and of all the quarrels that hang upon it. There is no end to those quarrels; for so long as there are two views in this country concerning freedom and slavery, so long, whatever party is in power, there will be quarrels concerning Executive appointments for the Territories; and not only concerning those, but concerning every act which those executive officers may do in the Territories. There will not only be quarrels here in Congress, and quarrels in all of the States, but there will be quarrels among the people of the Territories themselves ; for, sir, they enlist under party standards on the one side and the other, and no party, by any possibility, can ever attempt to do any thing that the other party cannot, will not, censure and condemn. There will be these constant partisan quarrels in the Territories, and they, with various reports of crimes, of murder and robbery, and arson, committed by Executive officials, or at their instigation, will be brought to the notice of this House, and parties here will range themselves upon the one side and upon the other, and we will have bitter, burning animosities, and never-ending disputes about this matter of non-resident jurisdiction.

This is a kind of government in no way consonant or consistent with our institutions. It never had any business under the stars and stripes. Now, sir, thank Heaven, it is ended. It has gone, once and forever, and we are no more to know it. Whatever we may annex hereafter, I say, let it be annexed as a sovereignty, and not as a dependency. We

have had enough of this history of dependencies. Let us have no more of it. I appeal to honest men in all parts of the House,—men who love the country more than they love prejudice, men who favor the institutions of the country more than they favor party,—now, once and for all, to settle this policy.

Sir, it was said by my colleague, with a sneer, that I had joined the Democratic party to-day in my vote. I say, that not only the Democratic party, but the American party, so far as I know, without an exception, and many of the gentlemen who act with me in the Republican party, voted to lay these bills upon the table. I tell you that, so far from being denounced for our action by the people, we shall be applauded, and the country will thank us, of whatever party, for having taken this perplexing question out of the halls of Congress. From this time we will enjoy the luxury of attending to the legitimate business of legislation.

I move that the bill be laid upon the table.

———

These comprise all of Mr. Thayer's public speeches as a member of Congress. The reader will observe that they discover a *practical* man. whose views are likewise consistent with the high abstract theories of government and progress under which we have become a great nation; and as such they demonstrate their author to be a Statesman. In the intervals of his public service and private occupations, Mr. Thayer has established a vigorous and thriving colony in Western Virginia, to which he has given the name of Ceredo. It does not lie within the compass of this publication to speak any further of this promising settlement than is necessary to set forth the varied energy of the man whose public life is herewith described. The plan of the establishment of Ceredo is precisely that by which Kansas was colonized, a town transplanted by the very simple machinery of Organized Emigration. By that process he has built up a large settlement in an unpopulated district, started a good newspaper, erected manufactories, school-houses, churches, and stores, given an impetus to agricultural and mechanical production, set up a hum of lively industry where solitude once reigned, and is making the desert smile like a garden. Nothing but Organized Emigration has accomplished it, operated by his clear head and energetic will

Ceredo enjoys the favor of the people of Western Virginia to a large extent. Mr. Thayer was told, at the start, that the population of that section would tolerate no such project; he went among them forthwith and laid his plan before them; he travelled into Eastern Kentucky with the same attractive story on his tongue; not only was he *not* opposed, or interfered with, by the people of that section, but they vied with one another in each locality with their friendly offers of reception! The tables were at once turned. When they found what a sensible, and safe, and altogether practical idea this of his was, — of Organized Emigration, — they accepted it with eagerness, feeling that it was the true key to their own salvation. He finally pitched upon a location in Wayne Co., Va., and purchased a tract of three thousand acres of second bottom land, two miles from Big Sandy, the western boundary of the State. The land here slopes down to the Ohio, and is adapted to the establishment of a city of the largest size. The Covington and Ohio R. R. finds its natural terminus here, and is to be a continuation of the Virginia Central. Another important railroad is also in contemplation, only seven miles below. The great advantages of the locality are in its resources of coal, timber, and iron, its mild climate, its railroad, and especially, its river navigation facilities. So great a change has been made in public opinion in Virginia, since he began the work of founding this new city, that at least fourteen of the State papers now openly advocate his scheme. Gov. Wise has given it his public approval, and no press says aught against it.

The speech on the Central American Question only foreshadowed the development of this same emigration plan of his, which followed upon the failure of the raid of Gen. Wm. Walker. The speech tells the whole story. Under the provisions of the Yrissarri treaty, American citizens were allowed to reside in Nicaragua, and enjoy the immunities granted to natives while still under the protection of their own government. San Juan del Norte and San Juan del Sud were to become free ports. Our merchants were to be allowed to introduce their goods on the same terms with the native merchants, and have the same rights and privileges. The inter-oceanic and native trade of Nicaragua, therefore, offered tempting inducements to our men of enterprise. All that Nicaragua wanted, was the infusion into its veins of the spirit of American thrift and energy. It is immensely fertile, its natural productions consisting of indigo, coffee, sugar, cocoa, rice, and cotton, the latter being of better quality than any produced in our Southern States; its fruits being oranges, lemons, plantains, and such other spontaneous growths as make the very name of the tropics delightful. Its chief source of wealth, however, is its cattle, large quantities of hides being exported.

Under a new spirit, Nicaragua may become a compact and powerful little commonwealth: and Mr. Eli Thayer saw it as quick as Gen. Walker did. But he would go to work to develop its resources, and make it a power, in a totally different way. The speech on Central America will tell the reader how the two men differed in their ideas, — the one being a Christian civilizer, the other only a barbarian fillibuster. Mr. Thayer set to work on this new problem of "Americanizing Central America" with his usual industry and resoluteness. He sent out a body of colonists to establish a post at the Gulf of Fonseca, on the Pacific coast. The stock to this enterprise was taken up eagerly, mostly by merchants of New York, who are engaged in Central American trade. From its favorable position, the colony will command a great part of the trade of Nicaragua, Honduras, and San Salvador, the population of these three States numbering about nine hundred thousand souls. The results to that region must be of the very last importance. With our own States, too, lying on the shores of the Atlantic and Pacific oceans, and the necessity that exists for the freest possible communication between them, this new emigration project of Mr. Thayer is pregnant with grand promises. Its very conception betrayed not more an active brain than a large one; not more shrewd practical plans than large and comprehensive ideas. While others were fussing and fretting over Walker, and it was likely that the entire country might be split into fillibusters and anti-fillibusters, Mr. Thayer comes forward and shows how the knot may be untied in a peaceful, civilized, and truly Christian manner. He drives such villains as Walker out of the field altogether. He shows us a new and better way to the accomplishment of manifest destiny; the road being lined with happy living beings, rather than strewn with the corpses of dead men. It is better to be an apostle than a pirate and fillibuster.

———

This is the place in which to insert extracts from the leading journals of the country, respecting the character of Mr. Eli Thayer's speeches, and his own character as a man and public servant. We quote into these pages, because such quotations are only a fair and necessary part of his biography. The St. Louis *Democrat* says of him: " He stands forth more the representative of the practical Yankee mind, out-cropping into sunnier provinces, than any other from the New England States. His modes are organisms; his ends, acquisitions: he gathers *the laurels of war with the appliances of peace!* ——— Says "SIGMA," in the Boston *Transcript*: " I have read your speech, Mr. Eli Thayer; I cannot come all the way to Washington, to thank you in person, but, as an humble citizen of Massachusetts, I thank you from the bottom of my heart; and, if I had you by the hand this moment, you would recognize the cordial grasp of a New Englander."——The Chicago *Press* says: " Mr. Thayer's entrance upon the political battle-ground of the two antagonistic social systems of this country is opportune, if not providential. He appears just at the time when Organized Emigration has become *essential to success.* * * * We cannot but regard him as one of the most remarkable men of the times."——The Boston *Daily Ledger* says: " A democrat in the *largest sense*, he is desirous that none but the popular cause shall prevail; that is, that numbers shall be heard over power and position. Such men will be in great demand in our immediate future as a nation."—— The Lawrence *Courier* says, speaking of the speech on Central America: " We admire it for its capacity *to stand alone.* It traverses an old field by a new path. It takes hold of slavery by a new handle. Under the whole of it is veiled an Americanism deeper and more pure, broader and more firm, than any thing which has ever yet gone by that name."—— Says the Albany *Evening Journal:* " You can have but a faint idea of the effect of Thayer's speech " (the one on Central America). —— Says the Worcester *Transcript:* " Mr. Thayer has already become a part of the history of our times, by his inauguration of this measure " (emigration).——The Kennebec, Me., *Journal* says: " He is a fit man to represent the heart of Massachusetts at this emergency in our political affairs. Original, independent, bold, determined, and able, he is as true to freedom as the needle to the pole, and will follow her flag wherever it may wave or need a standard-bearer."—— The Kansas *Herald of Freedom* says: "Mr. Thayer is one of the strong MEN of this country. He grasps readily the *strong* points of a proposition; he does not deal in abstractions, but in living, practical realities."—— Says the Boston *Atlas and Bee:* " Mr. Thayer, therefore, lays hold of squatter sovereignty as a means of preventing the extension of slavery into the Territories."——The Providence *Journal* says: " Some opposition has been manifested toward the re-nomination of Mr. Thayer, because he is in favor of directing the force of the Republican party to practical and present issues, rather than to abstract questions that will not rise again, and that are of no use, except to quarrel about."—— Says the Granite State (N. H.) *Whig:* " We glory in just such men as Eli Thayer: men of *work* as well as *words.*" We might extend these quotations almost indefinitely. They bespeak for the author of the foregoing speeches a consideration to which no mere politician, and certainly no ordinary man, could claim a title.

In the character of Eli Thayer are discovered certain fixed and marked traits, that would have made him a man of distinction wherever his lot might have been cast. In the first place, he has a forecaste, or high wisdom, that enables him, from the stand-point he occupies, to throw his observation far on into the future. He instinctively knows the *laws* of things, and therefore is not tossed about by the accidents of circumstances. Next, he is in the habit of taking a broad view of matters around him, and of placing them all in their right relation one to the other. Then he is possessed of a gift of native self-reliance, without which the others would be valueless. Seeing so clearly and so widely for himself, he abides strongly by the convictions that are thus formed. And he is a man of courage, too. He dare *announce* and *carry out* his convictions. Here is where so many of our public men fail. They lack just that one element, the main-spring of the whole, that keeps all the rest in motion. But what forms the top and crown of his character is his thorough truthfulness. He may be relied upon. In this regard, he reaches even a chivalric limit. His word is as clear as his perception. The sun shines through him, and his whole nature is transparent. And, finally, he is one of those rare persons, always in public demand, however, who has the faculty of *taking hold of things by the handle.* Somebody once protested to Daniel Webster that Mr. So-and-so certainly was no very great *lawyer,* and he wondered why so much was said of his ability at the bar. "I won't undertake to answer to *that,*" returned the great statesman, "but I know that *he always gets his cases.*" So with Eli Thayer; his enemies may stand about and dispute whether he has ability, judgment, logic, or what-not on his side, while he goes ahead himself and invariably "gets his cases." He is a successful man, because he sees things *as they are,* because he subordinates speculation and formalism to fact and practice. This is what makes him a successful teacher, a successful man of business, a successful legislator and a successful statesman. No man in New England to-day holds out a larger and truer promise than he.

But whether his walk tends in the direction of politics in the future, or in some other perhaps more congenial to his temper and tastes, it will remain as his monument that Eli Thayer invented and set in operation in this country, the system of ORGANIZED EMIGRATION; that to him chiefly, with the zealous and generous co-operation of such minds as Amos A. Lawrence, J. M. S. Williams, and Dr. Webb, is due the salvation and prosperity of Kansas; that he has taught the nation the magic secret of building up states in a day; and that, above all, FREE LABOR is both the cope and corner-stone of all our boasted institutions. Such a man the free laborers of this country will never refuse to honor. None can shake their confidence in his character.

As a leader in a powerful political party, the temper of Mr. Thayer may best be summed up in his own language: "Now, what should be the position of the Republican party in this conflict? Should it be that of a sneaking coward, running away from the slave power, and calling upon the rocks and mountains to cover us and hide us from that power which we fear is to overwhelm the world? No! It should be a *defiant position.* We should maintain a policy that is *positive,* and not *negative;* a policy which is aggressive, rather than yielding; a policy which is always on the advance: not a policy which makes us the mere tools to record the doings of some other party, but a policy which initiates measures and carries them out. I scorn to be a member of a party which is content to be nothing else than a writer of the history of some other party." * * *

"I scorn to be one of a party to be merely a herald at the Olympic games, and not *one of the conquerors.* I want the Republican party to be *the conquerors,* and not the herald to give *the name* of the conquerors." Such is the man's courage, boldness, and resolution. He is an advancing man, not one to throw obstacles in the way. He is an iconoclast, not an industrious picker up of the pieces. Whatever he has put his hand to, has thriven as by magic. He throws the magnetism of his energy into all his projects, and others catch the spirit and help render them successful.

REMARKS.

It is due to the subject of the foregoing sketch and author of the speeches, as well as to the reader of the within pages, to state that not a line or word of the same has been seen by Mr. Thayer, previous to publication in their present form, and that he has had no hand whatever in the work of compilation. The facts in his biography have been collected entirely from publications accessible to every one; a great many interesting details could have been secured, had the compiler thought proper—which he did not—to solicit them of Mr. Thayer himself. It is the aim of the present pamphlet merely to group together his Congressional Speeches, and interweave such a brief biographical sketch as any reader of the speeches would naturally call for; the one acting as a ready key to the other. It is believed that they are widely called for, both on account of the present position of public affairs and the career of the man.